From the library of

SOPHENE

Published by Sophene 2019

Scottish Tales was first published in 2019 by Sophene Pty Ltd.

These tales were originally edited and compiled by
Elizabeth Grierson and W. J. Glover.

www.sophenebooks.com

ISBN-13: 978-1-925937-20-6

SCOTTISH TALES

A COLLECTION OF CLASSIC SCOTTISH FOLK TALES

SCOTTISH TALES

A COLLECTION OF CLASSIC SCOTTISH FOLK TALES

CONTENTS

THE INHERITANCE

There was once a farmer who was well off. He had three sons. When he was on the bed of death he called them to him and said, "My sons, I am going to leave you; let there be no disputing when I am gone. In a certain drawer, in a dresser in the inner room, you will find a sum of gold; divide it fairly and honestly amongst you, work the farm, and live together as you have done with me," and shortly after the old man went away. The sons buried him, and when all was over they went to the drawer, and when they drew it out there was nothing in it.

They stood for a while without speaking a word. Then the youngest spoke:

"There is no knowing if there ever was any money at all."

"There was money, surely, wherever it is now," said the second; and the eldest said, "Our father never told a lie. There was money, certainly, though I cannot understand the matter. Come, let us go to such an old man; he was our father's friend; he knew him well; hew as at school with him; and no man knew so much of his affairs. Let us go to consult him."

So the brothers went to the house of the old man and told him all that had happened.

"Stay with me," said the old man, "and I will think over this matter. I cannot understand it; but, as you know, your father and I were very great with each other. When he had children I stood sponsor, and when I had children he did the same. I know that your father never told a lie." And he kept them there, and gave them meat and drink for ten days.

Then he sent for the three young lads, and he made them sit down beside him, and said:

"There was once a young lad, and he was poor, and he

fell in love with the daughter of a rich neighbor. The maiden loved him too, but because hew as so poor there could be no wedding. At least they pledged themselves toe ach other, and the young man went away and stayed in his own house. After a time there came another suitor, and because he was well-off, the girl's father made her promise to marry him, and after a time they were married. But directly afterwards the bride-groom found her weeping and bewailing. 'What ails thee?' he said. The brid would say nothing for a long time, then she told him all about it, and hos she had pledged herself to another. 'Dress thyself,' said the man, 'and follow me.' So she dressed herself in her wedding clothes, and he took the horse, and put her behind him, and rode to the house of the other man, leaving the bride there at the door while he returned home.

"What brought you here?" said he.

"'The main I married today. When I told him of the promise we had made he brought me here himself and left me.'

"Immediately he loosed the maiden from the promise she had given, and set her on the horse, telling her to return to her husband.

"So the bride rode away. She had not gone far when she came to a thick wood where three robbers topped and seized her.

"'Aha!' said one, "we have waited long, and have got nothing, but now we have the bride herself.'

"'Oh,' said she, 'let me go, let me go to my husband. Here are ten pounds in gold—take them, and let me go on my journey.' So she begged and prayed for a long time.

"At last one of the robbers, who was of a better nature than the rest, said, 'Come, I will take you home myself.'

"'Take thou the money,' said she.

"'I will not take a penny,' said the robber, but the other two said, 'Give us the money,' and they took the ten pounds.

"The maiden rode home, and the robber left her at her husband's door.

"Now," said the old man, "which of all these do you think did best?"

"I think the man that sent the maiden to him to whom she was pledged, was the honest, generous man," said the eldest son. "He did well."

The second said, "Yes, but the man to whom she was pledged did still better, when he sent her to her husband."

"Then," said the youngest, "I don't know myself; but perhaps the wisest of all were the robbers who got the money."

Then the old man rose up and said, "Thou hast thy father's gold and silver. I have kept you here for ten days. I have watched you well. I know your father never told a lie, and thou hast stolen the money." So the youngest son had to confess the fact, and the money was got and divided.

GOLD-TREE AND
SILVER-TREE

In bygone days there lived a little Princess named Gold-Tree, and she was one of the prettiest children in the whole world.

Although her mother was dead, she had a very happy life, for her father loved her dearly, and thought that nothing was too much trouble so long as it gave his little daughter pleasure. But by and by he married again, and then the little Princess's sorrows began.

For his new wife, whose name, curious to say, was Silver-Tree, was very beautiful, but she was also very jealous, and she made herself quite miserable for fear that, some day, she should meet someone who was better looking than she was herself.

When she found that her step-daughter was so very pretty, she took a dislike to her at once, and was always looking at her and wondering if people would think her prettier than she was. And because, in her heart of hearts, she was afraid that they would do so, she was very unkind indeed to the poor girl.

At last, one day, when Princess Gold-Tree was quite grown up, the two ladies went for a walk to a little well which lay, all surrounded by trees, in the middle of a deep glen.

Now the water in this well was so clear that everyone who looked into it saw his face reflected on the surface; and the proud Queen loved to come and peep into its depths, so that she could see her own picture mirrored in the water.

But to-day, as she was looking in, what should she see but a little trout, which was swimming quietly backwards and forwards not very far from the surface.

"Troutie, troutie, answer me this one question," said the

Queen. "Am not I the most beautiful woman in the world?"

"No, indeed, you are not," replied the trout promptly, jumping out of the water, as he spoke, in order to swallow a fly.

"Who is the most beautiful woman, then?" asked the disappointed Queen, for she had expected a far different answer.

"Thy step-daughter, the Princess Gold-Tree, without a doubt," said the little fish; then, frightened by the black look that came upon the jealous Queen's face, he dived to the bottom of the well.

It was no wonder that he did so, for the Queen's expression was not pleasant to look at, as she darted an angry glance at her fair young step-daughter, who was busy picking flowers some little distance away.

Indeed, she was so annoyed at the thought that anyone should say that the girl was prettier than she was, that she quite lost her self-control; and when she reached home she went up, in a violent passion, to her room, and threw herself on the bed, declaring that she felt very ill indeed.

It was in vain that Princess Gold-Tree asked her what the matter was, and if she could do anything for her. She would not let the poor girl touch her, but pushed her away as if she had been some evil thing. So at last the Princess had to leave her alone, and go out of the apartment, feeling very sad indeed.

By and by the King came home from his hunting, and he at once asked for the Queen. He was told that she had been seized with sudden illness, and that she was lying on her bed in her own room, and that no one, not even the Court Physician, who had been hastily summoned, could make out what was wrong with her.

In great anxiety—for he really loved her—the King went up to her bedside, and asked the Queen how she felt, and if there was anything that he could do to relieve her.

"Yes, there is one thing that thou couldst do," she answered harshly, "but I know full well that, even although it is the only thing that will cure me, thou wilt not do it."

"Nay," said the King, "I deserve better words at thy mouth than these; for thou knowest that I would give thee aught thou carest to ask, even if it be the half of my Kingdom."

"Then give me thy daughter's heart to eat," cried the Queen, "for unless I can obtain that, I will die, and that speedily."

She spoke so wildly, and looked at him in such a strange fashion, that the poor King really thought that her brain was turned, and he was at his wits' end what to do. He left the room, and paced up and down the corridor in great distress, until at last he remembered that that very morning the son of a great King had arrived from a country far over the sea, asking for his daughter's hand in marriage.

"Here is a way out of the difficulty," he said to himself. "This marriage pleaseth me well, and I will have it celebrated at once. Then, when my daughter is safe out of the country, I will send a lad up the hillside, and he shall kill a he-goat, and I will have its heart prepared and dressed, and send it up to my wife. Perhaps the sight of it will cure her of this madness."

So he had the strange Prince summoned before him, and told him how the Queen had taken a sudden illness that had wrought on her brain, and had caused her to take a dislike to the Princess, and how it seemed as if it would be a good thing if, with the maiden's consent, the marriage could take place at once, so that the Queen might be left alone to recover from her strange malady.

Now the Prince was delighted to gain his bride so easily, and the Princess was glad to escape from her step-mother's hatred, so the marriage took place at once, and the newly wedded pair set off across the sea for the Prince's country.

Then the King sent a lad up the hillside to kill a he-goat; and when it was killed he gave orders that its heart should be dressed and cooked, and sent to the Queen's apartment on a silver dish. And the wicked woman tasted it, believing it to be the heart of her step-daughter; and when she had done so, she rose from her bed and went about the Castle looking as well and hearty as ever.

I am glad to be able to tell you that the marriage of Princess Gold-Tree, which had come about in such a hurry, turned out to be a great success; for the Prince whom she had wedded was rich, and great, and powerful, and he loved her dearly, and she was as happy as the day was long.

So things went peacefully on for a year. Queen Silver-Tree was satisfied and contented, because she thought that her step-daughter was dead; while all the time the Princess was happy and prosperous in her new home.

But at the end of the year it chanced that the Queen went once more to the well in the little glen, in order to see her face reflected in the water.

And it chanced also that the same little trout was swimming backwards and forwards, just as he had done the year before. And the foolish Queen determined to have a better answer to her question this time than she had last.

"Troutie, troutie," she whispered, leaning over the edge of the well, "am not I the most beautiful woman in the world?"

"By my troth, thou art not," answered the trout, in his

very straightforward way.

"Who is the most beautiful woman, then?" asked the Queen, her face growing pale at the thought that she had yet another rival.

"Why, your Majesty's step-daughter, the Princess Gold-Tree, to be sure," answered the trout.

The Queen threw back her head with a sigh of relief. "Well, at any rate, people cannot admire her now," she said, "for it is a year since she died. I ate her heart for my supper."

"Art thou sure of that, your Majesty?" asked the trout, with a twinkle in his eye. "Methinks it is but a year since she married the gallant young Prince who came from abroad to seek her hand, and returned with him to his own country."

When the Queen heard these words she turned quite cold with rage, for she knew that her husband had deceived her; and she rose from her knees and went straight home to the Palace, and, hiding her anger as best she could, she asked him if he would give orders to have the Long Ship made ready, as she wished to go and visit her dear step-daughter, for it was such a very long time since she had seen her.

The King was somewhat surprised at her request, but he was only too glad to think that she had got over her hatred towards his daughter, and he gave orders that the Long Ship should be made ready at once.

Soon it was speeding over the water, its prow turned in the direction of the land where the Princess lived, steered by the Queen herself; for she knew the course that the boat ought to take, and she was in such haste to be at her journey's end that she would allow no one else to take the helm.

Now it chanced that Princess Gold-Tree was alone that day, for her husband had gone a-hunting. And as she looked out of one of the Castle windows she saw a boat coming sailing over the sea towards the landing place. She recognised it as her father's Long Ship, and she guessed only too well whom it carried on board.

She was almost beside herself with terror at the thought, for she knew that it was for no good purpose that Queen Silver-Tree had taken the trouble to set out to visit her, and she felt that she would have given almost anything she possessed if her husband had but been at home. In her distress she hurried into the servants' hall.

"Oh, what shall I do, what shall I do?" she cried, "for I see my father's Long Ship coming over the sea, and I know that my step-mother is on board. And if she hath a chance she will kill me, for she hateth me more than anything else upon earth."

Now the servants worshipped the ground that their young Mistress trod on, for she was always kind and considerate to them, and when they saw how frightened she was, and heard her piteous words, they crowded round her, as if to shield her from any harm that threatened her.

"Do not be afraid, your Highness," they cried; "we will defend thee with our very lives if need be. But in case thy Lady Step-Mother should have the power to throw any evil spell over thee, we will lock thee in the great Mullioned Chamber, then she cannot get nigh thee at all."

Now the Mullioned Chamber was a strong-room, which was in a part of the castle all by itself, and its door was so thick that no one could possibly break through it; and the Princess knew that if she were once inside the room, with its stout oaken door between her and her step-mother, she would be perfectly safe from any mischief that that wicked woman could devise.

So she consented to her faithful servants' suggestion, and allowed them to lock her in the Mullioned Chamber.

So it came to pass that when Queen Silver-Tree arrived at the great door of the Castle, and commanded the lackey who opened it to take her to his Royal Mistress, he told her, with a low bow, that that was impossible, because the Princess was locked in the strong-room of the Castle, and could not get out, because no one knew where the key was.

(Which was quite true, for the old butler had tied it round the neck of the Prince's favourite sheep-dog, and had sent him away to the hills to seek his master.)

"Take me to the door of the apartment," commanded the Queen. "At least I can speak to my dear daughter through it." And the lackey, who did not see what harm could possibly come from this, did as he was bid.

"If the key is really lost, and thou canst not come out to welcome me, dear Gold-Tree," said the deceitful Queen, "at least put thy little finger through the keyhole that I may kiss it."

The Princess did so, never dreaming that evil could come to her through such a simple action. But it did. For instead of kissing the tiny finger, her step-mother stabbed it with a poisoned needle, and, so deadly was the poison, that, before she could utter a single cry, the poor Princess fell, as one dead, on the floor.

When she heard the fall, a smile of satisfaction crept over Queen Silver-Tree's face. "Now I can say that I am the handsomest woman in the world," she whispered; and she went back to the lackey who stood waiting at the end of the passage, and told him that she had said all that she had to say to her daughter, and that now she must return home.

So the man attended her to the boat with all due cere-mony, and she set sail for her own country; and no one in the Castle knew that any harm had befallen their dear Mistress until the Prince came home from his hunting with the key of the Mullioned Chamber, which he had taken from his sheep-dog's neck, in his hand.

He laughed when he heard the story of Queen Sil-ver-Tree's visit, and told the servants that they had done well; then he ran upstairs to open the door and release his wife.

But what was his horror and dismay, when he did so, to find her lying dead at his feet on the floor.

He was nearly beside himself with rage and grief; and, because he knew that a deadly poison such as Queen Sil-ver-Tree had used would preserve the Princess's body so that it had no need of burial, he had it laid on a silken couch and left in the Mullioned Chamber, so that he could go and look at it whenever he pleased.

He was so terribly lonely, however, that in a little time he married again, and his second wife was just as sweet and as good as the first one had been. This new wife was very happy, there was only one little thing that caused her any trouble at all, and she was too sensible to let it make her miserable.

That one thing was that there was one room in the Cas-tle—a room which stood at the end of a passage by itself—which she could never enter, as her husband always carried the key. And as, when she asked him the reason of this, he always made an excuse of some kind, she made up her mind that she would not seem as if she did not trust him, so she asked no more questions about the matter.

But one day the Prince chanced to leave the door unlocked, and as he had never told her not to do so, she went in, and there she saw Princess Gold-Tree lying on the silken couch, looking as if she were asleep.

"Is she dead, or is she only sleeping?" she said to herself, and she went up to the couch and looked closely at the Princess. And there, sticking in her little finger, she discovered a curiously shaped needle.

"There hath been evil work here," she thought to herself. "If that needle be not poisoned, then I know naught of medicine." And, being skilled in leechcraft, she drew it carefully out.

In a moment Princess Gold-Tree opened her eyes and sat up, and presently she had recovered sufficiently to tell the Other Princess the whole story.

Now, if her step-mother had been jealous, the Other Princess was not jealous at all; for, when she heard all that had happened, she clapped her little hands, crying, "Oh, how glad the Prince will be; for although he hath married again, I know that he loves thee best."

That night the Prince came home from hunting looking very tired and sad, for what his second wife had said was quite true. Although he loved her very much, he was always mourning in his heart for his first dear love, Princess Gold-Tree.

"How sad thou art!" exclaimed his wife, going out to meet him. "Is there nothing that I can do to bring a smile to thy face?"

"Nothing," answered the Prince wearily, laying down his bow, for he was too heart-sore even to pretend to be gay.

"Except to give thee back Gold-Tree," said his wife mischievously. "And that can I do. Thou wilt find her alive and well in the Mullioned Chamber."

Without a word the Prince ran upstairs, and, sure enough, there was his dear Gold-Tree, sitting on the couch ready to welcome him.

He was so overjoyed to see her that he threw his arms round her neck and kissed her over and over again, quite forgetting his poor second wife, who had followed him upstairs, and who now stood watching the meeting that she had brought about.

She did not seem to be sorry for herself, however. "I always knew that thy heart yearned after Princess Gold-Tree," she said. "And it is but right that it should be so. For she was thy first love, and, since she hath come to life again, I will go back to mine own people."

"No, indeed thou wilt not," answered the Prince, "for it is thou who hast brought me this joy. Thou wilt stay with us, and we shall all three live happily together. And Gold-Tree and thee will become great friends."

And so it came to pass. For Princess Gold-Tree and the Other Princess soon became like sisters, and loved each other as if they had been brought up together all their lives.

In this manner another year passed away, and one evening, in the old country, Queen Silver-Tree went, as she had done before, to look at her face in the water of the little well in the glen.

And, as had happened twice before, the trout was there. "Troutie, troutie," she whispered, "am not I the most beautiful woman in the world?"

"By my troth, thou art not," answered the trout, as he had answered on the two previous occasions.

"And who dost thou say is the most beautiful woman now?" asked the Queen, her voice trembling with rage and vexation.

"I have given her name to thee these two years back," answered the trout. "The Princess Gold-Tree, of course."

"But she is dead," laughed the Queen. "I am sure of it this time, for it is just a year since I stabbed her little finger with a poisoned needle, and I heard her fall down dead on the floor."

"I would not be so sure of that," answered the trout, and without saying another word he dived straight down to the bottom of the well.

After hearing his mysterious words the Queen could not rest, and at last she asked her husband to have the Long Ship prepared once more, so that she could go and see her step-daughter.

The King gave the order gladly; and it all happened as it had happened before.

She steered the Ship over the sea with her own hands, and when it was approaching the land it was seen and recognised by Princess Gold-Tree.

The Prince was out hunting, and the Princess ran, in great terror, to her friend, the Other Princess, who was upstairs in her chamber.

"Oh, what shall I do, what shall I do?" she cried, "for I see my father's Long Ship coming, and I know that my cruel step-mother is on board, and she will try to kill me, as she tried to kill me before. Oh! come, let us escape to the hills."

"Not at all," replied the Other Princess, throwing her arms round the trembling Gold-Tree. "I am not afraid of thy Lady Step-Mother. Come with me, and we will go down to the sea shore to greet her."

So they both went down to the edge of the water, and when Queen Silver-Tree saw her step-daughter coming she pretended to be very glad, and sprang out of the boat and ran to meet her, and held out a silver goblet full of wine for her to drink.

"'Tis rare wine from the East," she said, "and therefore very precious. I brought a flagon with me, so that we might pledge each other in a loving cup."

Princess Gold-Tree, who was ever gentle and courteous, would have stretched out her hand for the cup, had not the Other Princess stepped between her and her step-mother.

"Nay, Madam," she said gravely, looking the Queen straight in the face; "it is the custom in this land for the one who offers a loving cup to drink from it first herself."

"I will follow the custom gladly," answered the Queen, and she raised the goblet to her mouth. But the Other Princess, who was watching for closely, noticed that she did not allow the wine that it contained to touch her lips. So she stepped forward and, as if by accident, struck the bottom of the goblet with her shoulder. Part of its contents flew into the Queen's face, and part, before she could shut her mouth, went down her throat.

So, because of her wickedness, she was, as the Good Book says, caught in her own net. For she had made the wine so poisonous that, almost before she had swallowed it, she fell dead at the two Princesses' feet.

No one was sorry for her, for she really deserved her fate; and they buried her hastily in a lonely piece of ground, and very soon everybody had forgotten all about her.

As for Princess Gold-Tree, she lived happily and peacefully with her husband and her friend for the remainder of her life.

WHIPPETY-STOURIE

I am going to tell you a story about a poor young widow woman, who lived in a house called Kittlerumpit, though whereabouts in Scotland the house of Kittlerumpit stood nobody knows.

Some folk think that it stood in the neighbourhood of the Debateable Land, which, as all the world knows, was on the Borders, where the old Border Reivers were constantly coming and going; the Scotch stealing from the English, and the English from the Scotch. Be that as it may, the widowed Mistress of Kittlerumpit was sorely to be pitied.

For she had lost her husband, and no one quite knew what had become of him. He had gone to a fair one day, and had never come back again, and although everybody believed that he was dead, no one knew how he died.

Some people said that he had been persuaded to enlist, and had been killed in the wars; others, that he had been taken away to serve as a sailor by the press-gang, and had been drowned at sea.

At any rate, his poor young wife was sorely to be pitied, for she was left with a little baby-boy to bring up, and, as times were bad, she had not much to live on.

But she loved her baby dearly, and worked all day amongst her cows, and pigs, and hens, in order to earn enough money to buy food and clothes for both herself and him.

Now, on the morning of which I am speaking, she rose very early and went out to feed her pigs, for rent-day was coming on, and she intended to take one of them, a great, big, fat creature, to the market that very day, as she thought that the price that it would fetch would go a long way towards paying her rent.

And because she thought so, her heart was light, and she hummed a little song to herself as she crossed the yard with her bucket on one arm and her baby-boy on the other.

But the song was quickly changed into a cry of despair when she reached the pig-stye, for there lay her cherished pig on its back, with its legs in the air and its eyes shut, just as if it were going to breathe its last breath.

"What shall I do? What shall I do?" cried the poor woman, sitting down on a big stone and clasping her boy to her breast, heedless of the fact that she had dropped her bucket, and that the pig's-meat was running out, and that the hens were eating it.

"First I lost my husband, and now I am going to lose my finest pig. The pig that I hoped would fetch a deal of money."

Now I must explain to you that the house of Kittlerumpit stood on a hillside, with a great fir wood behind it, and the ground sloping down steeply in front.

And as the poor young thing, after having a good cry to herself, was drying her eyes, she chanced to look down the hill, and who should she see coming up it but an Old Woman, who looked like a lady born.

She was dressed all in green, with a white apron, and she wore a black velvet hood on her head, and a steeple-crowned beaver hat over that, something like those, as I have heard tell, that the women wear in Wales. She walked very slowly, leaning on a long staff, and she gave a bit hirple now and then, as if she were lame.

As she drew near, the young widow felt it was becoming to rise and curtsey to the Gentlewoman, for such she saw her to be.

- 17 -

"Madam," she said, with a sob in her voice, "I bid you welcome to the house of Kittlerumpit, although you find its Mistress one of the most unfortunate women in the world."

"Hout-tout," answered the old Lady, in such a harsh voice that the young woman started, and grasped her baby tighter in her arms. "Ye have little need to say that. Ye have lost your husband, I grant ye, but there were waur losses at Shirra-Muir. And now your pig is like to die—I could, maybe, remedy that. But I must first hear how much ye wad gie me if I cured him."

"Anything that your Ladyship's Madam likes to ask," replied the widow, too much delighted at having the animal's life saved to think that she was making rather a rash promise.

"Very good," said the old Dame, and without wasting any more words she walked straight into the pig-sty.

She stood and looked at the dying creature for some minutes, rocking to and fro and muttering to herself in words which the widow could not understand; at least, she could only understand four of them, and they sounded something like this:

"Pitter-patter,
Haly water."

Then she put her hand into her pocket and drew out a tiny bottle with a liquid that looked like oil in it. She took the cork out, and dropped one of her long lady-like fingers into it; then she touched the pig on the snout and on his ears, and on the tip of his curly tail.

No sooner had she done so than up the beast jumped, and, with a grunt of contentment, ran off to its trough to look for its breakfast.

A joyful woman was the Mistress of Kittlerumpit when

she saw it do this, for she felt that her rent was safe; and in her relief and gratitude she would have kissed the hem of the strange Lady's green gown, if she would have allowed it, but she would not.

"No, no," said she, and her voice sounded harsher than ever. "Let us have no fine meanderings, but let us stick to our bargain. I have done my part, and mended the pig; now ye must do yours, and give me what I like to ask—your son."

Then the poor widow gave a piteous cry, for she knew now what she had not guessed before—that the Green-clad Lady was a Fairy, and a Wicked Fairy too, else had she not asked such a terrible thing.

It was too late now, however, to pray, and beseech, and beg for mercy; the Fairy stood her ground, hard and cruel.

"Ye promised me what I liked to ask, and I have asked your son; and your son I will have," she replied, "so it is useless making such a din about it. But one thing I may tell you, for I know well that the knowledge will not help you. By the laws of Fairy-land, I cannot take the bairn till the third day after this, and if by that time you have found out my name I cannot take him even then. But ye will not be able to find it out, of that I am certain. So I will call back for the boy in three days."

And with that she disappeared round the back of the pig-sty, and the poor mother fell down in a dead faint beside the stone.

All that day, and all the next, she did nothing but sit in her kitchen and cry, and hug her baby tighter in her arms; but on the day before that on which the Fairy said that she was coming back, she felt as if she must get a little breath of fresh air, so she went for a walk in the fir wood behind the house.

Now in this fir wood there was an old quarry hole, in the

bottom of which was a bonnie spring well, the water of which was always sweet and pure. The young widow was walking near this quarry hole, when, to her astonishment, she heard the whirr of a spinning-wheel and the sound of a voice lilting a song. At first she could not think where the sound came from; then, remembering the quarry, she laid down her child at a tree root, and crept noiselessly through the bushes on her hands and knees to the edge of the hole and peeped over.

She could hardly believe her eyes! For there, far below her, at the bottom of the quarry, beside the spring well, sat the cruel Fairy, dressed in her green frock and tall felt hat, spinning away as fast as she could at a tiny spinning-wheel.

And what should she be singing but—

"Little kens our guid dame at hame,
Whippety-Stourie is my name."

The widow woman almost cried aloud for joy, for now she had learned the Fairy's secret, and her child was safe. But she dare not, in case the wicked old Dame heard her and threw some other spell over her.

So she crept softly back to the place where she had left her child; then, catching him up in her arms, she ran through the wood to her house, laughing, and singing, and tossing him in the air in such a state of delight that, if anyone had met her, they would have been in danger of thinking that she was mad.

Now this young woman had been a merry-hearted maiden, and would have been merry-hearted still, if, since her marriage, she had not had so much trouble that it had made her grow old and sober-minded before her time; and she began to think what fun it would be to tease the Fairy for a few minutes before she let her know that she had found out her name.

So next day, at the appointed time, she went out with

her boy in her arms, and seated herself on the big stone where she had sat before; and when she saw the old Dame coming up the hill, she crumpled up her nice clean cap, and screwed up her face, and pretended to be in great distress and to be crying bitterly.

The Fairy took no notice of this, however, but came close up to her, and said, in her harsh, merciless voice, "Good wife of Kittlerumpit, ye ken the reason of my coming; give me the bairn."

Then the young mother pretended to be in sorer distress than ever, and fell on her knees before the wicked old woman and begged for mercy.

"Oh, sweet Madam Mistress," she cried, "spare me my bairn, and take, an' thou wilt, the pig instead."

"We have no need of bacon where I come from," answered the Fairy coldly; "so give me the laddie and let me be-gone—I have no time to waste in this wise."

"Oh, dear Lady mine," pleaded the Goodwife, "if thou wilt not have the pig, wilt thou not spare my poor bairn and take me myself?"

The Fairy stepped back a little, as if in astonishment. "Art thou mad, woman," she cried contemptuously, "that thou pro-posest such a thing? Who in all the world would care to take a plain-looking, red-eyed, dowdy wife like thee with them?"

Now the young Mistress of Kittlerumpit knew that she was no beauty, and the knowledge had never vexed her; but something in the Fairy's tone made her feel so angry that she could contain herself no longer.

"In troth, fair Madam, I might have had the wit to know that the like of me is not fit to tie the shoe-string of the High and Mighty Princess, WHIPPETY-STOURIE!"

If there had been a charge of gunpowder buried in the ground, and if it had suddenly exploded beneath her feet, the Wicked Fairy could not have jumped higher into air.

And when she came down again she simply turned round and ran down the brae, shrieking with rage and disappointment, for all the world, as an old book says, "like an owl chased by witches."

THE RED-ETIN

There were once two widows who lived in two cottages which stood not very far from one another. And each of those widows possessed a piece of land on which she grazed a cow and a few sheep, and in this way she made her living.

One of these poor widows had two sons, the other had one; and as these three boys were always together, it was natural that they should become great friends.

At last the time arrived when the eldest son of the widow who had two sons, must leave home and go out into the world to seek his fortune. And the night before he went away his mother told him to take a can and go to the well and bring back some water, and she would bake a cake for him to carry with him.

"But remember," she added, "the size of the cake will depend on the quantity of water that thou bringest back. If thou bringest much, then will it be large; and, if thou bringest little, then will it be small. But, big or little, it is all that I have to give thee."

The lad took the can and went off to the well, and filled it with water, and came home again. But he never noticed that the can had a hole in it, and was running out; so that, by the time that he arrived at home, there was very little water left. So his mother could only bake him a very little cake.

But, small as it was, she asked him, as she gave it to him, to choose one of two things. Either to take the half of it with her blessing, or the whole of it with her malison. "For," said she, "thou canst not have both the whole cake and a blessing along with it."

The lad looked at the cake and hesitated. It would have

been pleasant to have left home with his mother's blessing upon him; but he had far to go, and the cake was little; the half of it would be a mere mouthful, and he did not know when he would get any more food. So at last he made up his mind to take the whole of it, even if he had to bear his mother's malison.

Then he took his younger brother aside, and gave him his hunting-knife, saying, "Keep this by thee, and look at it every morning. For as long as the blade remains clear and bright, thou wilt know that it is well with me; but should it grow dim and rusty, then know thou that some evil hath befallen me."

After this he embraced them both and set out on his travels. He journeyed all that day, and all the next, and on the afternoon of the third day he came to where an old shepherd was sitting beside a flock of sheep.

"I will ask the old man whose sheep they are," he said to himself, "for mayhap his master might engage me also as a shepherd." So he went up to the old man, and asked him to whom the sheep belonged. And this was all the answer he got:

> *"The Red-Etin of Ireland*
> *Ance lived in Ballygan,*
> *And stole King Malcolm's daughter,*
> *The King of fair Scotland.*
> *He beats her, he binds her,*
> *He lays her on a band,*
> *And every day he dings her*
> *With a bright silver wand.*
> *Like Julian the Roman,*
> *He's one that fears no man.*

"It's said there's ane predestinate
To be his mortal foe,
But that man is yet unborn,
And lang may it be so."

"That does not tell me much; but somehow I do not fancy this Red-Etin for a master," thought the youth, and he went on his way.

He had not gone very far, however, when he saw another old man, with snow-white hair, herding a flock of swine; and as he wondered to whom the swine belonged, and if there was any chance of him getting a situation as a swineherd, he went up to the countryman, and asked who was the owner of the animals.

He got the same answer from the swineherd that he had got from the shepherd:

"The Red-Etin of Ireland
Ance lived in Ballygan,
And stole King Malcolm's daughter,
The King of fair Scotland.
He beats her, he binds her,
He lays her on a band,
And every day he dings her
With a bright silver wand.
Like Julian the Roman,
He's one that fears no man.

"It's said there's ane predestinate
To be his mortal foe,
But that man is yet unborn,

And lang may it be so."

"Plague on this old Red-Etin; I wonder when I will get out of his domains," he muttered to himself; and he journeyed still further.

Presently he came to a very, very old man—so old, indeed, that he was quite bent with age—and he was herding a flock of goats.

Once more the traveller asked to whom the animals belonged, and once more he got the same answer:

> *"The Red-Etin of Ireland*
> *Ance lived in Ballygan,*
> *And stole King Malcolm's daughter,*
> *The King of fair Scotland.*
> *He beats her, he binds her,*
> *He lays her on a band,*
> *And every day he dings her*
> *With a bright silver wand.*
> *Like Julian the Roman,*
> *He's one that fears no man.*
>
> *"It's said there's ane predestinate*
> *To be his mortal foe,*
> *But that man is yet unborn,*
> *And lang may it be so."*

But this ancient goatherd added a piece of advice at the end of his rhyme. "Beware, stranger," he said, "of the next herd of beasts that ye shall meet. Sheep, and swine, and goats will harm nobody; but the creatures ye shall now encounter are of a sort that ye have never met before, and *they* are not harmless."

The young man thanked him for his counsel, and went on his way, and he had not gone very far before he met a herd of very dreadful creatures, unlike anything that he had ever dreamed of in all his life.

For each of them had three heads, and on each of its three heads it had four horns; and when he saw them he was so frightened that he turned and ran away from them as fast as he could.

Up hill and down dale he ran, until he was well-nigh exhausted; and, just when he was beginning to feel that his legs would not carry him any further, he saw a great Castle in front of him, the door of which was standing wide open.

He was so tired that he went straight in, and after wandering through some magnificent halls, which appeared to be quite deserted, he reached the kitchen, where an old woman was sitting by the fire.

He asked her if he might have a night's lodging, as he had come a long and weary journey, and would be glad of somewhere to rest.

"You can rest here, and welcome, for me," said the old Dame, "but for your own sake I warn you that this is an ill house to bide in; for it is the Castle of the Red-Etin, who is a fierce and terrible Monster with three heads, and he spareth neither man nor woman, if he can get hold of them."

Tired as he was, the young man would have made an effort to escape from such a dangerous abode had he not remembered the strange and awful beasts from which he had just been fleeing, and he was afraid that, as it was growing dark, if he set out again he might chance to walk right into their midst. So he begged the old woman to hide him in some dark corner, and not to tell the Red-Etin that he was in the Castle.

"For," thought he, "if I can only get shelter until the morning, I will then be able to avoid these terrible creatures and go on my way in peace."

So the old Dame hid him in a press under the back stairs, and, as there was plenty of room in it, he settled down quite comfortably for the night.

But just as he was going off to sleep he heard an awful roaring and trampling overhead. The Red-Etin had come home, and it was plain that he was searching for something.

And the terrified youth soon found out what the "Something" was, for very soon the horrible Monster came into the kitchen, crying out in a voice like thunder:

"Seek but, and seek ben,
I smell the smell of an earthly man!
Be he living, or be he dead,
His heart this night I shall eat with my bread."

And it was not very long before he discovered the poor young man's hiding-place and pulled him roughly out of it.

Of course, the lad begged that his life might be spared, but the Monster only laughed at him.

"It will be spared if thou canst answer three questions," he said; "if not, it is forfeited."

The first of these three questions was, "Whether Ireland or Scotland was first inhabited?"

The second, "How old was the world when Adam was made?"

And the third, "Whether men or beasts were created first?"

The lad was not skilled in such matters, having had but little book-learning, and he could not answer the questions. So the Monster struck him on the head with a queer little hammer which he carried, and turned him into a piece of stone.

Now every morning since he had left home his younger brother had done as he had promised, and had carefully examined his hunting-knife.

On the first two mornings it was bright and clear, but on the third morning he was very much distressed to find that it was dull and rusty. He looked at it for a few moments in great dismay; then he ran straight to his mother, and held it out to her.

"By this token I know that some mischief hath befallen my brother," he said, "so I must set out at once to see what evil hath come upon him."

"First must thou go to the well and fetch me some water," said his mother, "that I may bake thee a cake to carry with thee, as I baked a cake for him who is gone. And I will say to thee what I said to him. That the cake will be large or small according as thou bringest much or little water back with thee."

So the lad took the can, as his brother had done, and went off to the well, and it seemed as if some evil spirit directed him to follow his example in all things, for he brought home little water, and he chose the whole cake and his mother's malison, instead of the half and her blessing, and he set out and met the shepherd, and the swineherd, and the goatherd, and they all gave the same answers to him which they had given to his brother. And he also encountered the same fierce beasts, and ran from them in terror, and took shelter from them in the

Castle; and the old woman hid him, and the Red-Etin found him, and, because he could not answer the three questions, he, too, was turned into a pillar of stone.

And no more would ever have been heard of these two youths had not a kind Fairy, who had seen all that had happened, appeared to the other widow and her son, as they were sitting at supper one night in the gloaming, and told them the whole story, and how their two poor young neighbours had been turned into pillars of stone by a cruel enchanter called Red-Etin.

Now the third young man was both brave and strong, and he determined to set out to see if he could in anywise help his two friends. And, from the very first moment that he had made up his mind to do so, things went differently with him than they had with them. I think, perhaps, that this was because he was much more loving and thoughtful than they were.

For, when his mother sent him to fetch water from the well so that she might bake a cake for him, just as the other mother had done for her sons, a raven, flying above his head, croaked out that his can was leaking, and he, wishing to please his mother by bringing her a good supply of water, patched up the hole with clay, and so came home with the can quite full.

Then, when his mother had baked a big bannock for him, and giving him his choice between the whole cake and her malison, or half of it and her blessing, he chose the latter, "for," said he, throwing his arms round her neck, "I may light on other cakes to eat, but I will never light on another blessing such as thine."

And the curious thing was, that, after he had said this, the half cake which he had chosen seemed to spread itself out, and widen, and broaden, till it was bigger by far than it had been at first.

Then he started on his journey, and, after he had gone a good way he began to feel hungry. So he pulled it out of his pocket and began to eat it.

Just then he met an old woman, who seemed to be very poor, for her clothing was thin, and worn, and old, and she stopped and spoke to him.

"Of thy charity, kind Master," she said, stretching out one of her withered hands, "spare me a bit of the cake that thou art eating."

Now the youth was very hungry, and he could have eaten it all himself, but his kind heart was touched by the woman's pinched face, so he broke it in two, and gave her half of it.

Instantly she was changed into the Fairy who had appeared to his mother and himself as they had sat at supper the night before, and she smiled graciously at the generous lad, and held out a little wand to him.

"Though thou knowest it not, thy mother's blessing and thy kindness to an old and poor woman hath gained thee many blessings, brave boy," he said. "Keep that as thy reward; thou wilt need it ere thy errand be done." Then, bidding him sit down on the grass beside her, she told him all the dangers that he would meet on his travels, and the way in which he could overcome them, and then, in a moment, before he could thank her, she vanished out of his sight.

But with the little wand, and all the instructions that she had given him, he felt that he could face fearlessly any danger that he might be called on to meet, so he rose from the grass and went his way, full of a cheerful courage.

After he had walked for many miles further, he came, as

each of his friends had done, to the old shepherd herding his sheep. And, like them, he asked to whom the sheep belonged. And this time the old man answered:

> *"The Red-Etin of Ireland*
> *Ance lived in Ballygan,*
> *And stole King Malcolm's daughter,*
> *The King of fair Scotland.*
> *He beats her, he binds her,*
> *He lays her on a band,*
> *And every day he dings her*
> *With a bright silver wand.*
> *Like Julian the Roman,*
> *He's one that fears no man.*
>
> *"But now I fear his end is near,*
> *And destiny at hand;*
> *And you're to be, I plainly see,*
> *The heir of all his land."*

Then the young man went on, and he came to the swineherd, and to the goatherd; and each of them in turn repeated the same words to him.

And, when he came to where the droves of monstrous beasts were, he was not afraid of them, and when one came running up to him with its mouth wide open to devour him, he just struck it with his wand, and it dropped down dead at his feet.

At last he arrived at the Red-Etin's Castle, and he knocked boldly at the door. The old woman answered his knock, and, when he had told her his errand, warned him gravely not to enter.

"Thy two friends came here before thee," she said, "and they are now turned into two pillars of stone; what advantage is it to thee to lose thy life also?"

But the young man only laughed. "I have knowledge of an art of which they knew nothing," he said. "And methinks I can fight the Red-Etin with his own weapons."

So, much against her will, the old woman let him in, and hid him where she had hid his friends.

It was not long before the Monster arrived, and, as on former occasions, he came into the kitchen in a furious rage, crying:

> "Seek but, and seek ben,
> I smell the smell of an earthly man!
> Be he living, or be he dead,
> His heart this night I shall eat with my bread."

Then he peered into the young man's hiding-place, and called to him to come out. And after he had come out, he put to him the three questions, never dreaming that he could answer them; but the Fairy had told the youth what to say, and he gave the answers as pat as any book.

Then the Red-Etin's heart sank within him for fear, for he knew that someone had betrayed him, and that his power was gone.

And gone in very truth it was. For when the youth took an axe and began to fight with him, he had no strength to resist, and, before he knew where he was, his heads were cut off. And that was the end of the Red-Etin.

As soon as he saw that his enemy was really dead, the

young man asked the old woman if what the shepherd, and the swineherd, and the goatherd had told him were true, and if King Malcolm's daughter were really a prisoner in the Castle.

The old woman nodded. "Even with the Monster lying dead at my feet, I am almost afraid to speak of it," she said. "But come with me, my gallant gentleman, and thou wilt see what dule and misery the Red-Etin hath caused to many a home."

She took a huge bunch of keys, and led him up a long flight of stairs, which ended in a passage with a great many doors on each side of it. She unlocked these doors with her keys, and, as she opened them, she put her head into every room and said, "Ye have naught to fear now, Madam, the Predestinated Deliverer hath come, and the Red-Etin is dead."

And behold, with a cry of joy, out of every room came a beautiful lady who had been stolen from her home, and shut up there, by the Red-Etin.

Among them was one who was more beautiful and stately than the rest, and all the others bowed down to her and treated her with such great reverence that it was clear to see that she was the Royal Princess, King Malcolm's daughter.

And when the youth stepped forward and did reverence to her also, she spoke so sweetly to him, and greeted him so gladly, and called him her Deliverer, in such a low, clear voice, that his heart was taken captive at once.

But, for all that, he did not forget his friends. He asked the old woman where they were, and she took him into a room at the end of the passage, which was so dark that one could scarcely see in it, and so low that one could scarcely stand upright.

In this dismal chamber stood two blocks of stone.

"One can unlock doors, young Master," said the old woman, shaking her head forebodingly, "but 'tis hard work to try to turn cauld stane back to flesh and blood."

"Nevertheless, I will do it," said the youth, and, lifting his little wand, he touched each of the stone pillars lightly on the top.

Instantly the hard stone seemed to soften and melt away, and the two brothers started into life and form again. Their gratitude to their friend, who had risked so much to save them, knew no bounds, while he, on his part, was delighted to think that his efforts had been successful.

The next thing to do was to convey the Princess and the other ladies (who were all noblemen's daughters) back to the King's Court, and this they did next day.

King Malcolm was so overjoyed to see his dearly loved daughter, whom he had given up for dead, safe and sound, and so grateful to her deliverer, that he said that he should become his son-in-law and marry the Princess, and come and live with them at Court. Which all came to pass in due time; while as for the two other young men, they married noblemen's daughters, and the two old mothers came to live near their sons, and everyone was as happy as they could possibly be.

THE SEAL CATCHER AND
THE MERMAN

Once upon a time there was a man who lived not very far from John o' Groat's house, which, as everyone knows, is in the very north of Scotland. He lived in a little cottage by the sea-shore, and made his living by catching seals and selling their fur, which is very valuable.

He earned a good deal of money in this way, for these creatures used to come out of the sea in large numbers, and lie on the rocks near his house basking in the sunshine, so that it was not difficult to creep up behind them and kill them.

Some of those seals were larger than others, and the country people used to call them "Roane," and whisper that they were not seals at all, but Mermen and Merwomen, who came from a country of their own, far down under the ocean, who assumed this strange disguise in order that they might pass through the water, and come up to breathe the air of this earth of ours.

But the seal catcher only laughed at them, and said that those seals were most worth killing, for their skins were so big that he got an extra price for them.

Now it chanced one day, when he was pursuing his calling, that he stabbed a seal with his hunting-knife, and whether the stroke had not been sure enough or not, I cannot say, but with a loud cry of pain the creature slipped off the rock into the sea, and disappeared under the water, carrying the knife along with it.

The seal catcher, much annoyed at his clumsiness, and also at the loss of his knife, went home to dinner in a very downcast frame of mind. On his way he met a horseman, who was so tall and so strange-looking and who rode on such a gigantic horse, that he stopped and looked at him in astonishment, wondering who he was, and from what country he came.

The stranger stopped also, and asked him his trade and on hearing that he was a seal catcher, he immediately ordered a great number of seal skins. The seal catcher was delighted, for such an order meant a large sum of money to him. But his face fell when the horseman added that it was absolutely necessary that the skins should be delivered that evening.

"I cannot do it," he said in a disappointed voice, "for the seals will not come back to the rocks again until to-morrow morning."

"I can take you to a place where there are any number of seals," answered the stranger, "if you will mount behind me on my horse and come with me."

The seal catcher agreed to this, and climbed up behind the rider, who shook his bridle rein, and off the great horse galloped at such a pace that he had much ado to keep his seat.

On and on they went, flying like the wind, until at last they came to the edge of a huge precipice, the face of which went sheer down to the sea. Here the mysterious horseman pulled up his steed with a jerk.

"Get off now," he said shortly.

The seal catcher did as he was bid, and when he found himself safe on the ground, he peeped cautiously over the edge of the cliff, to see if there were any seals lying on the rocks below.

To his astonishment he saw no rocks, only the blue sea, which came right up to the foot of the cliff.

"Where are the seals that you spoke of?" he asked anxiously, wishing that he had never set out on such a rash adventure.

"You will see presently," answered the stranger, who was attending to his horse's bridle.

The seal catcher was now thoroughly frightened, for he felt sure that some evil was about to befall him, and in such a lonely place he knew that it would be useless to cry out for help.

And it seemed as if his fears would prove only too true, for the next moment the stranger's hand was laid upon his shoulder, and he felt himself being hurled bodily over the cliff, and then he fell with a splash into the sea.

He thought that his last hour had come, and he wondered how anyone could work such a deed of wrong upon an innocent man.

But, to his astonishment, he found that some change must have passed over him, for instead of being choked by the water, he could breathe quite easily, and he and his companion, who was still close at his side, seemed to be sinking as quickly down through the sea as they had flown through the air.

Down and down they went, nobody knows how far, till at last they came to a huge arched door, which appeared to be made of pink coral, studded over with cockle-shells. It opened, of its own accord, and when they entered they found themselves in a huge hall, the walls of which were formed of mother-of-pearl, and the floor of which was of sea-sand, smooth, and firm, and yellow.

The hall was crowded with occupants, but they were seals, not men, and when the seal catcher turned to his companion to ask him what it all meant, he was aghast to find that he, too, had assumed the form of a seal. He was still more aghast when he caught sight of himself in a large mirror that hung on the wall, and saw that he also no longer bore the likeness of a man, but was transformed into a nice, hairy, brown seal.

"Ah, woe to me," he said to himself, "for no fault of mine own this artful stranger hath laid some baneful charm upon me, and in this awful guise will I remain for the rest of my natural life."

At first none of the huge creatures spoke to him. For some reason or other they seemed to be very sad, and moved gently about the hall, talking quietly and mournfully to one another, or lay sadly upon the sandy floor, wiping big tears from their eyes with their soft furry fins.

But presently they began to notice him, and to whisper to one another, and presently his guide moved away from him, and disappeared through a door at the end of the hall. When he returned he held a huge knife in his hand.

"Didst thou ever see this before?" he asked, holding it out to the unfortunate seal catcher, who, to his horror, recognised his own hunting knife with which he had struck the seal in the morning, and which had been carried off by the wounded animal.

At the sight of it he fell upon his face and begged for mercy, for he at once came to the conclusion that the inhabitants of the cavern, enraged at the harm which had been wrought upon their comrade, had, in some magic way, contrived to capture him, and to bring him down to their subterranean abode, in order to wreak their vengeance upon him by killing him.

But, instead of doing so, they crowded round him, rubbing their soft noses against his fur to show their sympathy, and implored him not to put himself about, for no harm would befall him, and they would love him all their lives long if he would only do what they asked him.

"Tell me what it is," said the seal catcher, "and I will do it, if it lies within my power."

"Follow me," answered his guide, and he led the way to the door through which he had disappeared when he went to seek the knife.

The seal catcher followed him. And there, in a smaller room, he found a great brown seal lying on a bed of pale pink sea-weed, with a gaping wound in his side.

"That is my father," said his guide, "whom thou wounded this morning, thinking that he was one of the common seals who live in the sea, instead of a Merman who hath speech, and understanding, as you mortals have. I brought thee hither to bind up his wounds, for no other hand than thine can heal him."

"I have no skill in the art of healing," said the seal catcher, astonished at the forbearance of these strange creatures, whom he had so unwittingly wronged; "but I will bind up the wound to the best of my power, and I am only sorry that it was my hands that caused it."

He went over to the bed, and, stooping over the wounded Merman, washed and dressed the hurt as well as he could; and the touch of his hands appeared to work like magic, for no sooner had he finished than the wound seemed to deaden and die, leaving only the scar, and the old seal sprang up, as well as ever.

Then there was great rejoicing throughout the whole Palace of the Seals. They laughed, and they talked, and they embraced each other in their own strange way, crowding round their comrade, and rubbing their noses against his, as if to show him how delighted they were at his recovery.

But all this while the seal catcher stood alone in a corner, with his mind filled with dark thoughts, for although he saw now that they had no intention of killing him, he did not relish the prospect of spending the rest of his life in the guise of a seal, fathoms deep under the ocean.

But presently, to his great joy, his guide approached him, and said, "Now you are at liberty to return home to your wife and children. I will take you to them, but only on one condition."

"And what is that?" asked the seal catcher eagerly, overjoyed at the prospect of being restored safely to the upper world, and to his family.

"That you will take a solemn oath never to wound a seal again."

"That will I do right gladly," he replied, for although the promise meant giving up his means of livelihood, he felt that if only he regained his proper shape he could always turn his hand to something else.

So he took the required oath with all due solemnity, holding up his fin as he swore, and all the other seals crowded round him as witnesses. And a sigh of relief went through the halls when the words were spoken, for he was the most noted seal catcher in the North.

Then he bade the strange company farewell, and, accompanied by his guide, passed once more through the outer doors of coral, and up, and up, and up, through the shadowy green water, until it began to grow lighter and lighter and at last they emerged into the sunshine of earth.

Then, with one spring, they reached the top of the cliff, where the great black horse was waiting for them, quietly nibbling the green turf.

When they left the water their strange disguise dropped from them, and they were now as they had been before, a plain seal catcher and a tall, well-dressed gentleman in riding clothes.

"Get up behind me," said the latter, as he swung himself into his saddle. The seal catcher did as he was bid, taking tight hold of his companion's coat, for he remembered how nearly he had fallen off on his previous journey.

Then it all happened as it happened before. The bridle was shaken, and the horse galloped off, and it was not long before the seal catcher found himself standing in safety before his own garden gate.

He held out his hand to say "good-bye," but as he did so the stranger pulled out a huge bag of gold and placed it in it.

"Thou hast done thy part of the bargain—we must do ours," he said. "Men shall never say that we took away an honest man's work without making reparation for it, and here is what will keep thee in comfort to thy life's end."

Then he vanished, and when the astonished seal catcher carried the bag into his cottage, and turned the gold out on the table, he found that what the stranger had said was true, and that he would be a rich man for the remainder of his days.

THE PAGE-BOY AND THE SILVER GOBLET

There was once a little page-boy, who was in service in a stately Castle. He was a very good-natured little fellow, and did his duties so willingly and well that everybody liked him, from the great Earl whom he served every day on bended knee, to the fat old butler whose errands he ran.

Now the Castle stood on the edge of a cliff overlooking the sea, and although the walls at that side were very thick, in them there was a little postern door, which opened on to a narrow flight of steps that led down the face of the cliff to the sea shore, so that anyone who liked could go down there in the pleasant summer mornings and bathe in the shimmering sea.

On the other side of the Castle were gardens and pleasure grounds, opening on to a long stretch of heather-covered moorland, which, at last, met a distant range of hills.

The little page-boy was very fond of going out on this moor when his work was done, for then he could run about as much as he liked, chasing bumble-bees, and catching butterflies, and looking for birds' nests when it was nesting time.

And the old butler was very pleased that he should do so, for he knew that it was good for a healthy little lad to have plenty of fun in the open air. But before the boy went out the old man always gave him one warning.

"Now, mind my words, laddie, and keep far away from the Fairy Knowe, for the Little Folk are not to trust to."

This Knowe of which he spoke was a little green hillock, which stood on the moor not twenty yards from the garden gate, and folk said that it was the abode of Fairies, who would punish any rash mortal who came too near them. And because of this the country people would walk a good half-mile out of their way, even in broad daylight, rather than run the risk of going too near the Fairy Knowe and bringing down the Little Folks' displeasure upon them. And at night they would hardly cross the moor at all, for everyone knows that Fairies come abroad in the darkness, and the door of their dwelling stands open, so that any luckless mortal who does not take care may find himself inside.

Now, the little page-boy was an adventurous wight, and instead of being frightened of the Fairies, he was very anxious to see them, and to visit their abode, just to find out what it was like.

So one night, when everyone else was asleep, he crept out of the Castle by the little postern door, and stole down the stone steps, and along the sea shore, and up on to the moor, and went straight to the Fairy Knowe.

To his delight he found that what everyone said was true. The top of the Knowe was tipped up, and from the opening that was thus made, rays of light came streaming out.

His heart was beating fast with excitement, but, gathering his courage, he stooped down and slipped inside the Knowe.

He found himself in a large room lit by numberless tiny candles, and there, seated round a polished table, were scores of the Tiny Folk, Fairies, and Elves, and Gnomes, dressed in green, and yellow, and pink; blue, and lilac, and scarlet; in all the colours, in fact, that you can think of.

He stood in a dark corner watching the busy scene in wonder, thinking how strange it was that there should be such a number of these tiny beings living their own lives all unknown to men, at such a little distance from them, when suddenly someone—he could not tell who it was—gave an order.

"Fetch the Cup," cried the owner of the unknown voice, and instantly two little Fairy pages, dressed all in scarlet livery, darted from the table to a tiny cupboard in the rock, and returned staggering under the weight of a most beautiful silver cup, richly embossed and lined inside with gold.

He placed it in the middle of the table, and, amid clapping of hands and shouts of joy, all the Fairies began to drink out of it in turn. And the page could see, from where he stood, that no one poured wine into it, and yet it was always full, and that the wine that was in it was not always the same kind, but that each Fairy, when he grasped its stem, wished for the wine that he loved best, and lo! in a moment the cup was full of it.

"'Twould be a fine thing if I could take that cup home with me," thought the page. "No one will believe that I have been here except I have something to show for it." So he bided his time, and watched.

Presently the Fairies noticed him, and, instead of being angry at his boldness in entering their abode, as he expected that they would be, they seemed very pleased to see him, and invited him to a seat at the table. But by and by they grew rude and insolent, and jeered at him for being content to serve mere mortals, telling him that they saw everything that went on at the Castle, and making fun of the old butler, whom the page loved with all his heart. And they laughed at the food he ate, saying that it was only fit for animals; and when any fresh dainty was set on the table by the scarlet-clad pages, they would push the dish across to him, saying: "Taste it, for you will not have the chance of tasting such things at the Castle."

At last he could stand their teasing remarks no longer;

besides, he knew that if he wanted to secure the cup he must lose no time in doing so.

So he suddenly stood up, and grasped the stem of it tightly in his hand. "I'll drink to you all in water," he cried, and instantly the ruby wine was turned to clear cold water.

He raised the cup to his lips, but he did not drink from it. With a sudden jerk he threw the water over the candles, and instantly the room was in darkness. Then, clasping the precious cup tightly in his arms, he sprang to the opening of the Knowe, through which he could see the stars glimmering clearly.

He was just in time, for it fell to with a crash behind him; and soon he was speeding along the wet, dew-spangled moor, with the whole troop of Fairies at his heels. They were wild with rage, and from the shrill shouts of fury which they uttered, the page knew well that, if they overtook him, he need expect no mercy at their hands.

And his heart began to sink, for, fleet of foot though he was, he was no match for the Fairy Folk, who gained on him steadily.

All seemed lost, when a mysterious voice sounded out of the darkness:

> *"If thou wouldst gain the Castle door,*
> *Keep to the black stones on the shore."*

It was the voice of some poor mortal, who, for some reason or other, had been taken prisoner by the Fairies—who were really very malicious Little Folk—and who did not want a like fate to befall the adventurous page-boy; but the little fellow did not know this.

He had once heard that if anyone walked on the wet sands, where the waves had come over them, the Fairies could not touch him, and this mysterious sentence brought the saying into his mind.

So he turned, and dashed panting down to the shore. His feet sank in the dry sand, his breath came in little gasps, and he felt as if he must give up the struggle; but he persevered, and at last, just as the foremost Fairies were about to lay hands on him, he jumped across the water-mark on to the firm, wet sand, from which the waves had just receded, and then he knew that he was safe.

For the Little Folk could go no step further, but stood on the dry sand uttering cries of rage and disappointment, while the triumphant page-boy ran safely along the shore, his precious cup in his arms, and climbed lightly up the steps in the rock and disappeared through the postern. And for many years after, long after the little page-boy had grown up and become a stately butler, who trained other little page-boys to follow in his footsteps, the beautiful cup remained in the Castle as a witness of his adventure.

THE BLACK BULL OF NORROWAY

In bygone days, long centuries ago, there lived a widowed Queen who had three daughters. And this widowed Queen was so poor, and had fallen upon such evil days, that she and her daughters had often much ado to get enough to eat.

So the eldest Princess determined that she would set out into the world to seek her fortune. And her mother was quite willing that she should do so. "For," said she, "'tis better to work abroad than to starve at home."

But as there was an old hen-wife living near the Castle who was said to be a witch, and to be able to foretell the future, the Queen sent the Princess to her cottage, before she set out on her travels, to ask her in which of the Four Airts she ought to go, in order to find the best fortune.

"Thou needst gang nae farther than my back door, hinnie," answered the old Dame, who had always felt very sorry for the Queen and her pretty daughters, and was glad to do them a good turn.

So the Princess ran through the passage to the hen-wife's back door and peeped out, and what should she see but a magnificent coach, drawn by six beautiful cream-coloured horses, coming along the road.

Greatly excited at this unusual sight, she hurried back to the kitchen, and told the hen-wife what she had seen.

"Aweel, aweel, ye've seen your fortune," said the old woman, in a tone of satisfaction, "for that coach-and-six is coming for thee."

Sure enough, the coach-and-six stopped at the gate of the Castle, and the second Princess came running down to the cottage to tell her sister to make haste, because it was waiting for her. Delighted beyond measure at the wonderful luck that had come to her, she hurried home, and, saying farewell to her mother and sisters, took her seat within, and the horses galloped off immediately.

And I've heard tell that they drew her to the Palace of a great and wealthy Prince, who married her; but that is outside my story.

A few weeks afterwards, the second Princess thought that she would do as her sister had done, and go down to the hen-wife's cottage, and tell her that she, too, was going out into the world to seek her fortune. And, of course, in her heart of hearts she hoped that what had happened to her sister would happen to her also.

And, curious to say, it did. For the old hen-wife sent her to look out at her back door, and she went, and, lo and behold! another coach-and-six was coming along the road. And when she went and told the old woman, she smiled upon her kindly, and told her to hurry home, for the coach-and-six was her fortune also, and that it had come for her.

So she, too, ran home, and got into her grand carriage, and was driven away. And, of course, after all these lucky happenings, the youngest Princess was anxious to try what her fortune might be; so the very night, in high good humour, she tripped away down to the old witch's cottage.

She, too, was told to look out at the back door, and she was only too glad to do so; for she fully expected to see a third coach-and-six coming rolling along the high road, straight for the Castle door.

But, alas and alack! no such sight greeted her eager eyes, for the high road was quite deserted, and in great disappointment she ran back to the hen-wife to tell her so.

"Then it is clear that thy fortune is not coming to meet thee this day," said the old Dame, "so thou must e'en come back to-morrow."

So the little Princess went home again, and next day she turned up once more at the old wife's cottage.

But once more she was disappointed, for although she looked out long and eagerly, no glad sight of a coach-and-six, or of any other coach, greeted her eyes. On the third day, however, what should she see but a great Black Bull coming rushing along the road, bellowing as it came, and tossing its head fiercely in the air.

In great alarm, the little Princess shut the door, and ran to the hen-wife to tell her about the furious animal that was approaching.

"Hech, hinnie," cried the old woman, holding up her hands in dismay, "and who would have thocht that the Black Bull of Norroway wad be your fate!"

At the words, the poor little maiden grew pale. She had come out to seek her fortune, but it had never dawned upon her that her fortune could be anything so terrible as this.

"But the Bull cannot be my fortune," she cried in terror. "I cannot go away with a bull."

"But ye'll need tae," replied the hen-wife calmly. "For you lookit out of my door with the intent of meeting your fortune; and when your fortune has come tae ye, you must just thole it."

And when the poor Princess ran weeping to her mother, to beg to be allowed to stay at home, she found her mother of the same mind as the Wise Woman; and so she had to allow herself to be lifted up on to the back of the enormous Black

Bull that had come up to the door of the Castle, and was now standing there quietly enough. And when she was settled, he set off again on his wild career, while she sobbed and trembled with terror, and clung to his horns with all her might.

On and on they went, until at last the poor maiden was so faint with fear and hunger that she could scarce keep her seat.

Just as she was losing her hold of the great beast's horns, however, and feeling that she must fall to the ground, he turned his massive head round a little, and, speaking in a wonderfully soft and gentle voice, said: "Eat out of my right ear, and drink out of my left ear, so wilt thou be refreshed for thy journey."

So the Princess put a trembling hand into the Bull's right ear, and drew out some bread and meat, which, in spite of her terror, she was glad to swallow; then she put her hand into his left ear, and found there a tiny flagon of wine, and when she had drunk that, her strength returned to her in a wonderful way.

Long they went, and sore they rode, till, just as it seemed to the Princess that they must be getting near the World's End, they came in sight of a magnificent Castle.

"That's where we maun bide this night," said the Black Bull of Norroway, "for that is the house of one of my brothers."

The Princess was greatly surprised at these words; but by this time she was too tired to wonder very much at anything, so she did not answer, but sat still where she was, until the Bull ran into the courtyard of the Castle and knocked his great head against the door.

The door was opened at once by a very splendid footman, who treated the Black Bull with great respect, and helped the Princess to alight from his back. Then he ushered her into a magnificent hall, where the Lord of the Castle, and his Lady, and a great and noble company were assembled; while the Black Bull trotted off quite contentedly to the grassy park which stretched all round the building, to spend the night there.

The Lord and his Lady were very kind to the Princess, and gave her her supper, and led her to a richly furnished bedroom, all hung round with golden mirrors, and left her to rest there; and in the morning, just as the Black Bull came trotting up to the front door, they handed her a beautiful apple, telling her not to break it, but to put it in her pocket, and keep it till she was in the greatest strait that mortal could be in. Then she was to break it, and it would bring her out of it.

So she put the apple in her pocket, and they lifted her once more on to the Black Bull's back, and she and her strange companion continued on their journey.

All that day they travelled, far further than I can tell you, and at night they came in sight of another Castle, which was even bigger and grander than the first.

"That's where we maun bide this night," said the Black Bull, "for that is the home of another of my brothers."

And here the Princess rested for the night in a very fine bedroom indeed, all hung with silken curtains; and the Lord and Lady of the Castle did everything to please her and make her comfortable.

And in the morning, before she left, they presented her with the largest pear that she had ever seen, and warned her that she must not break it until she was in the direst strait that she had ever been in, and then, if she broke it, it would bring her out of it.

The third day was the same as the other two had been.

The Princess and the Black Bull of Norroway rode many a weary mile, and at sundown they came to another Castle, more splendid by far than the other two.

This Castle belonged to the Black Bull's youngest brother, and here the Princess abode all night; while the Bull, as usual, lay outside in the park. And this time, when they departed, the Princess received a most lovely plum, with the warning not to break it till she was in the greatest strait that mortal could be in. Then she was to break it, and it would set her free.

On the fourth day, however, things were changed. For there was no fine Castle waiting for them at the end of their journey; on the contrary, as the shadows began to lengthen, they came to a dark, deep glen, which was so gloomy and so awesome-looking that the poor Princess felt her courage sinking as they approached it.

At the entrance the Black Bull stopped. "Light down here, Lady," he said, "for in this glen a deadly conflict awaits me, which I must face unaided and alone. For the dark and gloomy region that lies before us is the abode of a great Spirit of Darkness, who worketh much ill in the world. I would fain fight with him and overcome him; and, by my troth, I have good hope that I shall do so. As for thee, thou must seat thyself on this stone, and stir neither hand, nor foot, nor tongue till I return. For, if thou but so much as move, then the Evil Spirit of the Glen will have thee in his power."

"But how shall I know what is happening to thee?" asked the Princess anxiously, for she was beginning to grow quite fond of the huge black creature that had carried her so gallantly these last four days, "if I have neither to move hand nor foot, nor yet to speak."

"Thou wilt know by the signs around thee," answered the

Bull. "For if everything about thee turn blue, then thou wilt know that I have vanquished the Evil Spirit; but if everything about thee turn red, then the Evil Spirit hath vanquished me."

With these words he departed, and was soon lost to sight in the dark recesses of the glen, leaving the little Princess sitting motionless on her stone, afraid to move so much as her little finger, in case some unknown evil fell upon her.

At last, when she had sat there for well-nigh an hour, a curious change began to pass over the landscape. First it turned grey, and then it turned a deep azure blue, as if the sky had descended on the earth.

"The Bull hath conquered," thought the Princess. "Oh! what a noble animal he is!" And in her relief and delight she moved her position and crossed one leg over the other.

Oh, woe-a-day! In a moment a mystic spell fell upon her, which caused her to become invisible to the eyes of the Prince of Norroway, who, having vanquished the Evil Spirit, was loosed from the spell which had lain over him, and had transformed him into the likeness of a great Black Bull, and who returned in haste down the glen to present himself, in his rightful form, to the maiden whom he loved, and whom he hoped to win for his bride.

Long, long he sought, but he could not find her, while all the time she was sitting patiently waiting on the stone; but the spell was on her eyes also, and hindered her seeing him, as it hindered him seeing her.

So she sat on and on, till at last she became so wearied, and lonely, and frightened, that she burst out crying, and cried herself to sleep; and when she woke in the morning she felt that it was no use sitting there any longer, so she rose and took her way, hardly knowing whither she was going.

And she went, and she went, till at last she came to a great hill made all of glass, which blocked her way and prevented her going any further. She tried time after time to climb it, but it was all of no avail, for the surface of the hill was so slippery that she only managed to climb up a few feet, to slide down again the next moment.

So she began to walk round the bottom of the hill, in the hope of finding some path that would lead her over it, but the hill was so big, and she was so tired, that it seemed almost a hopeless quest, and her spirit died completely within her. And as she went slowly along, sobbing with despair, she felt that if help did not come soon she must lie down and die.

About mid-day, however, she came to a little cottage, and beside the cottage there was a smithy, where an old smith was working at his anvil.

She entered, and asked him if he could tell her of any path that would lead her over the mountain. The old man laid down his hammer and looked at her, slowly shaking his head as he did so.

"Na, na, lassie," he said, "there is no easy road over the Mountain of Glass. Folk maun either walk round it, which is not an easy thing to do, for the foot of it stretches out for hundreds of miles, and the folk who try to do so are almost sure to lose their way; or they maun walk over the top of it, and that can only be done by those who are shod with iron shoon."

"And how am I to get these iron shoon?" cried the Princess eagerly. "Couldst thou fashion me a pair, good man? I would gladly pay thee for them." Then she stopped suddenly, for she remembered that she had no money.

"These shoon cannot be made for siller," said the old man solemnly. "They can only be earned by service. I alone can make them, and I make them for those who are willing to serve me."

"And how long must I serve thee ere thou makest them for me?" asked the Princess faintly.

"Seven years," replied the old man, "for they be magic shoon, and that is the magic number."

So, as there seemed nothing else for it, the Princess hired herself to the smith for seven long years: to clean his house, and cook his food, and make and mend his clothes.

At the end of that time he fashioned her a pair of iron shoon, with which she climbed the Mountain of Glass with as much ease as if it had been covered with fresh green turf.

When she had reached the summit, and descended to the other side, the first house that she came to was the house of an old washerwoman, who lived there with her only daughter. And as the Princess was now very tired, she went up to the door, and knocked, and asked if she might be allowed to rest there for the night.

The washerwoman, who was old and ugly, with a sly and evil face, said that she might—on one condition—and that was that she should try to wash a white mantle that the Black Knight of Norroway had brought to her to wash, as he had got it stained in a deadly fight.

"Yestreen I spent the lee-long day washing it," went on the old Dame, "and I might as well have let it lie on the table. For at night, when I took it out of the wash-tub, the stains were there as dark as ever. Peradventure, maiden, if thou wouldst try thy hand upon it thou mightest be more successful. For I am loth to disappoint the Black Knight of Norroway, who is an exceeding great and powerful Prince."

"Is he in any way connected with the Black Bull of

Norroway?" asked the Princess; for at the name her heart had leaped for joy, for it seemed that mayhap she was going to find once more him whom she had lost.

The old woman looked at her suspiciously. "The two are one," she answered; "for the Black Knight chanced to have a spell thrown over him, which turned him into a Black Bull, and which could not be lifted until he had fought with, and overcome, a mighty Spirit of Evil that lived in a dark glen. He fought with the Spirit, and overcame it and once more regained his true form; but 'tis said that his mind is somewhat clouded at times, for he speaketh ever of a maiden whom he would fain have wedded, and whom he hath lost. Though who, or what she was, no living person kens. But this story can have no interest to a stranger like thee," she added slowly, as if she were sorry for having said so much. "I have no more time to waste in talking. But if thou wilt try and wash the mantle, thou art welcome to a night's lodging; and if not, I must ask thee to go on thy way."

Needless to say, the Princess said that she would try to wash the mantle; and it seemed as if her fingers had some magic power in them, for as soon as she put it into water the stains vanished, and it became as white and clean as when it was new.

Of course, the old woman was delighted, but she was very suspicious also, for it appeared to her that there must be some mysterious link between the maiden and the Knight, if his mantle became clean so easily when she washed it, when it had remained soiled and stained in spite of all the labour which she and her daughter had bestowed upon it.

So, as she knew that the young Gallant intended returning for it that very night, and as she wanted her daughter to get the credit of washing it, she advised the Princess to go to bed early, in order to get a good night's rest after all her labours. And the Princess followed her advice, and thus it came about that she was sound asleep, safely hidden in the big box-bed in the corner, when the Black Knight of Norroway came to the cottage to claim his white mantle.

Now you must know that the young man had carried about this mantle with him for the last seven years—ever since his encounter with the Evil Spirit of the Glen—always trying to find someone who could wash it for him, and never succeeding.

For it had been revealed to him by a wise woman that she who could make it white and clean was destined to be his wife—be she bonnie or ugly, old or young. And that, moreover, she would prove a loving, a faithful, and a true helpmeet.

So when he came to the washerwoman's cottage, and received back his mantle white as the driven snow, and heard that it was the washerwoman's daughter who had wrought this wondrous change, he said at once that he would marry her, and that the very next day.

When the Princess awoke in the morning and heard all that had befallen, and how the Black Knight had come to the cottage while she was asleep, and had received his mantle, and had promised to marry the washerwoman's daughter that very day, her heart was like to break. For now she felt that she never would have the chance of speaking to him and telling him who she really was.

And in her sore distress she suddenly remembered the beautiful fruit which she had received on her journey seven long years before, and which she had carried with her ever since.

"Surely I will never be in a sorer strait than I am now," she said to herself; and she drew out the apple and broke it. And, lo and behold! it was filled with the most beautiful precious stones that she had ever seen; and at the sight of them a plan came suddenly into her head.

She took the precious stones out of the apple, and, putting them into a corner of her kerchief, carried them to the washerwoman.

"See," said she, "I am richer than mayhap thou thoughtest I was. And if thou wilt, all these riches may be thine."

"And how could that come about?" asked the old woman eagerly, for she had never seen so many precious stones in her life before, and she had a great desire to become the possessor of them.

"Only put off thy daughter's wedding for one day," replied the Princess. "And let me watch beside the Black Knight as he sleeps this night, for I have long had a great desire to see him."

To her astonishment the washerwoman agreed to this request; for the wily old woman was very anxious to get the jewels, which would make her rich for life, and it did not seem to her that there was any harm in the Princess's request; for she had made up her mind that she would give the Black Knight a sleeping-draught, which would effectually prevent him as much as speaking to this strange maiden.

So she took the jewels and locked them up in her kist, and the wedding was put off, and that night the little Princess slipped into the Black Knight's apartment when he was asleep, and watched all through the long hours by his bedside, singing this song to him in the hope that he would awake and hear it:

"Seven lang years I served for thee,
The glassy hill I clamb for thee.
The mantle white I washed for thee,
And wilt thou no waken, and turn to me?"

But although she sang it over and over again, as if her heart would burst, he neither listened nor stirred, for the old washerwoman's potion had made sure of that.

Next morning, in her great trouble, the little Princess broke open the pear, hoping that its contents would help her better than the contents of the apple had done. But in it she found just what she had found before—a heap of precious stones; only they were richer and more valuable than the others had been.

So, as it seemed the only thing to do, she carried them to the old woman, and bribed her to put the wedding off for yet another day, and allow her to watch that night also by the Black Prince's bedside.

And the washerwoman did so; "for," said she, as she locked away the stones, "I shall soon grow quite rich at this rate."

But, alas! it was all in vain that the Princess spent the long hours singing with all her might:

"Seven lang years I served for thee,
The glassy hill I clamb for thee,
The mantle white I washed for thee,
And wilt thou no waken, and turn to me?"

for the young Prince whom she watched so tenderly,

remained deaf and motionless as a stone.

By the morning she had almost lost hope, for there was only the plum remaining now, and if that failed her last chance had gone. With trembling fingers she broke it open, and found inside another collection of precious stones, richer and rarer than all the others.

She ran with these to the washerwoman, and, throwing them into her lap, told her she could keep them all and welcome if she would put off the wedding once again, and let her watch by the Prince for one more night. And, greatly wondering, the old woman consented.

Now it chanced that the Black Knight, tired with waiting for his wedding, went out hunting that day with all his attendants behind him. And as the servants rode they talked together about something that had puzzled them sorely these two nights gone by. At last an old huntsman rode up to the Knight, with a question upon his lips.

"Master," he said, "we would fain ken who the sweet singer is who singeth through the night in thy chamber?"

"Singer!" he repeated. "There is no singer. My chamber hath been as quiet as the grave, and I have slept a dreamless sleep ever since I came to live at the cottage."

The old huntsman shook his head. "Taste not the old wife's draught this night, Master," he said earnestly; "then wilt thou hear what other ears have heard."

At other times the Black Knight would have laughed at his words, but to-day the man spoke with such earnestness that he could not but listen to them. So that evening, when the washerwoman, as was her wont, brought his sleeping-draught of spiced ale to his bedside, he told her that it was not sweet enough for his liking. And when she turned and went to the kitchen to fetch some honey to sweeten it, he jumped out of bed and poured it all out of the window, and when she came back he pretended that he had drunk it.

So it came to pass that he lay awake that night and heard the Princess enter his room, and listened to her plaintive little song, sung in a voice that was full of sobs:

> *"Seven lang years I served for thee,*
> *The glassy hill I clamb for thee,*
> *The mantle white I washed for thee,*
> *And wilt thou no waken, and turn to me?"*

And when he heard it, he understood it all; and he sprang up and took her in his arms and kissed her, and asked her to tell him the whole story.

And when he heard it, he was so angry with the old washerwoman and her deceitful daughter that he ordered them to leave the country at once; and he married the little Princess, and they lived happily all their days.

THE WEE BANNOCK

"Some tell about their sweethearts,
How they tirled them to the winnock,
But I'll tell you a bonnie tale
About a guid oatmeal bannock."

There was once an old man and his wife, who lived in a dear little cottage by the side of a burn. They were a very canty and contented couple, for they had enough to live on, and enough to do. Indeed, they considered themselves quite rich, for, besides their cottage and their garden, they possessed two sleek cows, five hens and a cock, an old cat, and two kittens.

The old man spent his time looking after the cows, and the hens, and the garden; while the old woman kept herself busy spinning.

One day, just after breakfast, the old woman thought that she would like an oatmeal bannock for her supper that evening, so she took down her bakeboard, and put on her girdle, and baked a couple of fine cakes, and when they were ready she put them down before the fire to harden.

While they were toasting, her husband came in from the byre, and sat down to take a rest in his great arm-chair. Presently his eyes fell on the bannocks, and, as they looked very good, he broke one through the middle and began to eat it.

When the other bannock saw this it determined that it should not have the same fate, so it ran across the kitchen and out of the door as fast as it could. And when the old woman saw it disappearing, she ran after it as fast as her legs would carry her, holding her spindle in one hand and her distaff in the other.

But she was old, and the bannock was young, and it ran faster than she did, and escaped over the hill behind the house. It ran, and it ran, and it ran, until it came to a large newly thatched cottage, and, as the door was open, it took refuge inside, and ran right across the floor to a blazing fire, which was burning in the first room that it came to.

Now, it chanced that this house belonged to a tailor, and he and his two apprentices were sitting cross-legged on the top of a big table by the window, sewing away with all their might, while the tailor's wife was sitting beside the fire carding lint.

When the wee bannock came trundling across the floor, all three tailors got such a fright that they jumped down from the table and hid behind the Master Tailor's wife.

"Hoot," she said, "what a set of cowards ye be! 'Tis but a nice wee bannock. Get hold of it and divide it between you, and I'll fetch you all a drink of milk."

So she jumped up with her lint and her lint cards, and the tailor jumped up with his great shears, and one apprentice grasped the line measure, while another took up the saucer full of pins; and they all tried to catch the wee bannock. But it dodged them round and round the fire, and at last it got safely out of the door and ran down the road, with one of the apprentices after it, who tried to snip it in two with his shears.

It ran too quickly for him, however, and at last he stopped and went back to the house, while the wee bannock ran on until it came to a tiny cottage by the roadside. It trundled in at the door, and there was a weaver sitting at his loom, with his wife beside him, winding a clue of yarn.

"What's that, Tibby?" said the weaver, with a start as the little cake flew past him.

"Oh!" cried she in delight, jumping to her feet, "'tis a wee bannock. I wonder where it came from?"

"Dinna bother your head about that, Tibby," said her man, "but grip it, my woman, grip it."

But it was not so easy to get hold of the wee bannock. It was in vain that the Goodwife threw her clue at it, and that the Goodman tried to chase it into a corner and knock it down with his shuttle. It dodged, and turned, and twisted, like a thing bewitched, till at last it flew out at the door again, and vanished down the hill, "for all the world," as the old woman said, "like a new tarred sheep, or a daft cow."

In the next house that it came to it found the Goodwife in the kitchen, kirning. She had just filled her kirn, and there was still some cream standing in the bottom of her cream jar.

"Come away, little bannock," she cried when she saw it. "Thou art come in just the nick of time, for I am beginning to feel hungry, and I'll have cakes and cream for my dinner."

But the wee bannock hopped round to the other side of the kirn, and the Goodwife after it. And she was in such a hurry that she nearly upset the kirn; and by the time that she had put it right again, the wee bannock was out at the door and half-way down the brae to the mill.

The miller was sifting meal in the trough, but he straightened himself up when he saw the little cake.

"It's a sign of plenty when bannocks are running about with no one to look after them," he said; "but I like bannocks and cheese, so just come in, and I will give thee a night's lodging."

But the little bannock had no wish to be eaten up by the miller, so it turned and ran out of the mill, and the miller was so busy that he did not trouble himself to run after it.

After this it ran on, and on, and on, till it came to the smithy, and it popped in there to see what it could see.

The smith was busy at the anvil making horse-shoe nails, but he looked up as the wee bannock entered.

"If there be one thing I am fond of, it is a glass of ale and a well-toasted cake," he cried. "So come inbye here, and welcome to ye."

But as soon as the little bannock heard of the ale, it turned and ran out of the smithy as fast as it could, and the disappointed smith picked up his hammer and ran after it. And when he saw that he could not catch it, he flung his heavy hammer at it, in the hope of knocking it down, but, luckily for the little cake, he missed his aim.

After this the bannock came to a farmhouse, with a great stack of peats standing at the back of it. In it went, and ran to the fireside. In this house the master had all the lint spread out on the floor, and was cloving[1] it with an iron rod, while the mistress was heckling[2] what he had already cloven.

"Oh, Janet," cried the Goodman in surprise, "here comes in a little bannock. It looks rare and good to eat. I'll have one half of it."

"And I'll have the other half," cried the Goodwife. "Hit it over the back with your cloving-stick, Sandy, and knock it down. Quick, or it will be out at the door again."

But the bannock played "jook-about," and dodged behind a chair. "Hoot!" cried Janet contemptuously, for she thought that her husband might easily have hit it, and she threw her heckle at it.

But the heckle missed it, just as her husband's cloving-rod had done, for it played "jook-about" again, and flew

[1] Separating the lint from the stalk.
[2] Combing.

out of the house.

This time it ran up a burnside till it came to a little cottage standing among the heather.

Here the Goodwife was making porridge for the supper in a pot over the fire, and her husband was sitting in a corner plaiting ropes of straw with which to tie up the cow.

"Oh, Jock! come here, come here," cried the Goodwife. "Thou art aye crying for a little bannock for thy supper; come here, histie, quick, and help me to catch it."

"Ay, ay," assented Jock, jumping to his feet and hurrying across the little room. "But where is it? I cannot see it."

"There, man, there," cried his wife, "under that chair. Run thou to that side; I will keep to this."

So Jock ran into the dark corner behind the chair; but, in his hurry, he tripped and fell, and the wee bannock jumped over him and flew laughing out at the door.

Through the whins and up the hillside it ran, and over the top of the hill, to a shepherd's cottage on the other side.

The inmates were just sitting down to their porridge, and the Goodwife was scraping the pan.

"Save us and help us," she exclaimed, stopping with the spoon half-way to her mouth. "There's a wee bannock come in to warm itself at our fireside."

"Sneck the door," cried the husband, "and we'll try to catch it. It would come in handy after the porridge."

But the bannock did not wait until the door was sneckit. It turned and ran as fast as it could, and the shepherd and his wife and all the bairns ran after it, with their spoons in their hands, in hopes of catching it.

And when the shepherd saw that it could run faster than they could, he threw his bonnet at it, and almost struck it; but it escaped all these dangers, and soon it came to another house, where the folk were just going to bed.

The Goodman was half undressed, and the Goodwife was raking the cinders carefully out of the fire.

"What's that?" said he, "for the bowl of brose that I had at supper-time wasna' very big."

"Catch it, then," answered his wife, "and I'll have a bit, too. Quick! quick! Throw your coat over it or it will be away."

So the Goodman threw his coat right on the top of the little bannock, and almost managed to smother it; but it struggled bravely, and got out, breathless and hot, from under it. Then it ran out into the grey light again, for night was beginning to fall, and the Goodman ran out after it, without his coat. He chased it and chased it through the stackyard and across a field, and in amongst a fine patch of whins. Then he lost it; and, as he was feeling cold without his coat, he went home.

As for the poor little bannock, it thought that it would creep under a whin bush and lie there till morning, but it was so dark that it never saw that there was a fox's hole there. So it fell down the fox's hole, and the fox was very glad to see it, for he had had no food for two days.

"Oh, welcome, welcome," he cried; and he snapped it through the middle with his teeth, and that was the end of the poor wee bannock.

And if a moral be wanted for this tale, here it is: That people should never be too uplifted or too cast down over anything, for all the good folk in the story thought that they were going to get the bannock, and, lo and behold! the fox got it after all.

THE ELFIN KNIGHT

There is a lone moor in Scotland, which, in times past, was said to be haunted by an Elfin Knight. This Knight was only seen at rare intervals, once in every seven years or so, but the fear of him lay on all the country round, for every now and then someone would set out to cross the moor and would never be heard of again.

And although men might search every inch of the ground, no trace of him would be found, and with a thrill of horror the searching party would go home again, shaking their heads and whispering to one another that he had fallen into the hands of the dreaded Knight.

So, as a rule, the moor was deserted, for nobody dare pass that way, much less live there; and by and by it became the haunt of all sorts of wild animals, which made their lairs there, as they found that they never were disturbed by mortal huntsmen.

Now in that same region lived two young earls, Earl St. Clair and Earl Gregory, who were such friends that they rode, and hunted, and fought together, if need be.

And as they were both very fond of the chase, Earl Gregory suggested one day that they should go a-hunting on the haunted moor, in spite of the Elfin King.

"Certes, I hardly believe in him at all," cried the young man, with a laugh. "Methinks 'tis but an old wife's tale to frighten the bairns withal, lest they go straying amongst the heather and lose themselves. And 'tis pity that such fine sport should be lost because we—two bearded men—pay heed to such gossip."

But Earl St. Clair looked grave. "'Tis ill meddling with unchancy things," he answered, "and 'tis no bairn's tale that travellers have set out to cross that moor who have vanished bodily, and never mair been heard of; but it is, as thou sayest, a pity that so much good sport be lost, all because an Elfin Knight choosest to claim the land as his, and make us mortals pay toll for the privilege of planting a foot upon it.

"I have heard tell, however, that one is safe from any power that the Knight may have if one wearest the Sign of the Blessed Trinity. So let us bind That on our arm and ride forth without fear."

Sir Gregory burst into a loud laugh at these words. "Dost thou think that I am one of the bairns," he said, "'first to be frightened by an idle tale, and then to think that a leaf of clover will protect me? No, no, carry that Sign if thou wilt; I will trust to my good bow and arrow."

But Earl St. Clair did not heed his companion's words, for he remembered how his mother had told him, when he was a little lad at her knee that whoso carried the Sign of the Blessed Trinity need never fear any spell that might be thrown over him by Warlock or Witch, Elf or Demon.

So he went out to the meadow and plucked a leaf of clover, which he bound on his arm with a silken scarf; then he mounted his horse and rode with Earl Gregory to the desolate and lonely moorland.

For some hours all went well; and in the heat of the chase the young men forgot their fears. Then suddenly both of them reined in their steeds and sat gazing in front of them with affrighted faces.

For a horseman had crossed their track, and they both

would fain have known who he was and whence he came.

"By my troth, but he rideth in haste, whoever he may be," said Earl Gregory at last, "and tho' I always thought that no steed on earth could match mine for swiftness, I reckon that for every league that mine goeth, his would go seven. Let us follow him, and see from what part of the world he cometh."

"The Lord forbid that thou shouldst stir thy horse's feet to follow him," said Earl St. Clair devoutly. "Why, man, 'tis the Elfin Knight! Canst thou not see that he doth not ride on the solid ground, but flieth through the air, and that, although he rideth on what seemeth a mortal steed, he is really craried by mighty pinions, which cleave the air like those of a bird? Follow him forsooth! It will be an evil day for thee when thou seekest to do that."

But Earl St. Clair forgot that he carried a Talisman which his companion lacked, that enabled him to see things as they really were, while the other's eyes were holden, and he was startled and amazed when Earl Gregory said sharply, "Thy mind hath gone mad over this Elfin King. I tell thee he who passed was a goodly Knight, clad in a green vesture, and riding on a great black jennet. And because I love a gallant horseman, and would fain learn his name and degree, I will follow him till I find him, even if it be at the world's end."

And without another word he put spurs to his horse and galloped off in the direction which the mysterious stranger had taken, leaving Earl St. Clair alone upon the moorland, his fingers touching the sacred Sign and his trembling lips muttering prayers for protection.

For he knew that his friend had been bewitched, and he made up his mind, brave gentleman that he was, that he would follow him to the world's end, if need be, and try to deliver him from the spell that had been cast over him.

Meanwhile Earl Gregory rode on and on, ever following in the wake of the Knight in green, over moor, and burn, and moss, till he came to the most desolate region that he had ever been in in his life; where the wind blew cold, as if from snowfields, and where the hoar-frost lay thick and white on the withered grass at his feet.

And there, in front of him, was a sight from which mortal man might well shrink back in awe and dread. For he saw an enormous Ring marked out on the ground, inside of which the grass, instead of being withered and frozen, was lush, and rank, and green, where hundreds of shadowy Elfin figures were dancing, clad in loose transparent robes of dull blue, which seemed to curl and twist round their wearers like snaky wreaths of smoke.

These weird Goblins were shouting and singing as they danced, and waving their arms above their heads, and throwing themselves about on the ground, for all the world as if they had gone mad; and when they saw Earl Gregory halt on his horse just outside the Ring they beckoned to him with their skinny fingers.

"Come hither, come hither," they shouted; "come tread a measure with us, and afterwards we will drink to thee out of our Monarch's loving cup."

And, strange as it may seem, the spell that had been cast over the young Earl was so powerful that, in spite of his fear, he felt that he must obey the eldrich summons, and he threw his bridle on his horse's neck and prepared to join them.

But just then an old and grizzled Goblin stepped out

from among his companions and approached him.

Apparently he dare not leave the charmed Circle, for he stopped at the edge of it; then, stooping down and pretending to pick up something, he whispered in a hoarse whisper:

"I know not whom thou art, nor from whence thou comest, Sir Knight, but if thou lovest thy life, see to it that thou comest not within this Ring, nor joinest with us in our feast. Else wilt thou be for ever undone."

But Earl Gregory only laughed. "I vowed that I would follow the Green Knight," he replied, "and I will carry out my vow, even if the venture leadeth me close to the nethermost world."

And with these words he stepped over the edge of the Circle, right in amongst the ghostly dancers.

At his coming they shouted louder than ever, and danced more madly, and sang more lustily; then, all at once, a silence fell upon them, and they parted into two companies, leaving a way through their midst, up which they signed to the Earl to pass.

He walked through their ranks till he came to the middle of the Circle; and there, seated at a table of red marble, was the Knight whom he had come so far to seek, clad in his grass-green robes. And before him, on the table, stood a wondrous goblet, fashioned from an emerald, and set round the rim with blood-red rubies.

And this cup was filled with heather ale, which foamed up over the brim; and when the Knight saw Sir Gregory, he lifted it from the table, and handed it to him with a stately bow, and Sir Gregory, being very thirsty, drank.

And as he drank he noticed that the ale in the goblet

never grew less, but ever foamed up to the edge; and for the first time his heart misgave him, and he wished that he had never set out on this strange adventure.

But, alas! the time for regrets had passed, for already a strange numbness was stealing over his limbs, and a chill pallor was creeping over his face, and before he could utter a single cry for help the goblet dropped from his nerveless fingers, and he fell down before the Elfin King like a dead man.

Then a great shout of triumph went up from all the company; for if there was one thing which filled their hearts with joy, it was to entice some unwary mortal into their Ring and throw their uncanny spell over him, so that he must needs spend long years in their company.

But soon their shouts of triumphs began to die away, and they muttered and whispered to each other with looks of something like fear on their faces.

For their keen ears heard a sound which filled their hearts with dread. It was the sound of human footsteps, which were so free and untrammelled that they knew at once that the stranger, whoever he was, was as yet untouched by any charm. And if this were so he might work them ill, and rescue their captive from them.

And what they dreaded was true; for it was the brave Earl St. Clair who approached, fearless and strong because of the Holy Sign he bore.

And as soon as he saw the charmed Ring and the eldrich dancers, he was about to step over its magic border, when the little grizzled Goblin who had whispered to Earl Gregory, came and whispered to him also.

"Alas! alas!" he exclaimed, with a look of sorrow on his wrinkled face, "hast thou come, as thy companion came, to pay thy toll of years to the Elfin King? Oh! if thou hast wife or child behind thee, I beseech thee, by all that thou holdest sacred, to turn back ere it be too late."

"Who art thou, and from whence hast thou come?" asked the Earl, looking kindly down at the little creature in front of him.

"I came from the country that thou hast come from," wailed the Goblin. "For I was once a mortal man, even as thou. But I set out over the enchanted moor, and the Elfin King appeared in the guise of a beauteous Knight, and he looked so brave, and noble, and generous that I followed him hither, and drank of his heather ale, and now I am doomed to bide here till seven long years be spent.

"As for thy friend, Sir Earl, he, too, hath drunk of the accursed draught, and he now lieth as dead at our lawful Monarch's feet. He will wake up, 'tis true, but it will be in such a guise as I wear, and to the bondage with which I am bound."

"Is there naught that I can do to rescue him!" cried Earl St. Clair eagerly, "ere he taketh on him the Elfin shape? I have no fear of the spell of his cruel captor, for I bear the Sign of One Who is stronger than he. Speak speedily, little man, for time presseth."

"There is something that thou couldst do, Sir Earl," whispered the Goblin, "but to essay it were a desperate attempt. For if thou failest, then could not even the Power of the Blessed Sign save thee."

"And what is that?" asked the Earl impatiently.

"Thou must remain motionless," answered the old man,

"in the cold and frost till dawn break and the hour cometh when they sing Matins in the Holy Church. Then must thou walk slowly nine times round the edge of the enchanted Circle, and after that thou must walk boldly across it to the red marble table where sits the Elfin King. On it thou wilt see an emerald goblet studded with rubies and filled with heather ale. That must thou secure and carry away; but whilst thou art doing so let no word cross thy lips. For this enchanted ground whereon we dance may look solid to mortal eyes, but in reality it is not so. 'Tis but a quaking bog, and under it is a great lake, wherein dwelleth a fearsome Monster, and if thou so much as utter a word while thy foot resteth upon it, thou wilt fall through the bog and perish in the waters beneath."

So saying the Grisly Goblin stepped back among his companions, leaving Earl St. Clair standing alone on the outskirts of the charmed Ring.

There he waited, shivering with cold, through the long, dark hours, till the grey dawn began to break over the hill tops, and, with its coming, the Elfin forms before him seemed to dwindle and fade away.

And at the hour when the sound of the Matin Bell came softly pealing from across the moor, he began his solemn walk. Round and round the Ring he paced, keeping steadily on his way, although loud murmurs of anger, like distant thunder, rose from the Elfin Shades, and even the very ground seemed to heave and quiver, as if it would shake this bold intruder from its surface.

But through the power of the Blessed Sign on his arm Earl St. Clair went on unhurt.

When he had finished pacing round the Ring he stepped

boldly on to the enchanted ground, and walked across it; and what was his astonishment to find that all the ghostly Elves and Goblins whom he had seen, were lying frozen into tiny blocks of ice, so that he was sore put to it to walk amongst them without treading upon them.

And as he approached the marble table the very hairs rose on his head at the sight of the Elfin King sitting behind it, stiff and stark like his followers; while in front of him lay the form of Earl Gregory, who had shared the same fate.

Nothing stirred, save two coal-black ravens, who sat, one on each side of the table, as if to guard the emerald goblet, flapping their wings, and croaking hoarsely.

When Earl St. Clair lifted the precious cup, they rose in the air and circled round his head, screaming with rage, and threatening to dash it from his hands with their claws; while the frozen Elves, and even their mighty King himself stirred in their sleep, and half sat up, as if to lay hands on this presumptuous intruder. But the Power of the Holy Sign restrained them, else had Earl St. Clair been foiled in his quest.

As he retraced his steps, awesome and terrible were the sounds that he heard around him. The ravens shrieked, and the frozen Goblins screamed; and up from the hidden lake below came the sound of the deep breathing of the awful Monster who was lurking there, eager for prey.

But the brave Earl heeded none of these things, but kept steadily onwards, trusting in the Might of the Sign he bore. And it carried him safely through all the dangers; and just as the sound of the Matin Bell was dying away in the morning air he stepped on to solid ground once more, and flung the enchanted goblet from him.

And lo! every one of the frozen Elves vanished, along with their King and his marble table, and nothing was left on the rank green grass save Earl Gregory, who slowly woke from his enchanted slumber, and stretched himself, and stood up, shaking in every limb. He gazed vaguely round him, as if he scarce remembered where he was.

And when, after Earl St. Clair had run to him and had held him in his arms till his senses returned and the warm blood coursed through his veins, the two friends returned to the spot where Earl St. Clair had thrown down the wondrous goblet, they found nothing but a piece of rough grey whinstone, with a drop of dew hidden in a little crevice which was hollowed in its side.

HABETROT THE SPINSTRESS

In bygone days, in an old farmhouse that stood by a river, there lived a beautiful girl called Maisie. She was tall and straight, with auburn hair and blue eyes, and she was the prettiest girl in all the valley. And one would have thought that she would have been the pride of her mother's heart.

But, instead of this, her mother used to sigh and shake her head whenever she looked at her. And why?

Because, in those days, all men were sensible; and instead of looking out for pretty girls to be their wives, they looked out for girls who could cook and spin, and who gave promise of becoming notable housewives.

Maisie's mother had been an industrious spinster; but, alas! to her sore grief and disappointment, her daughter did not take after her.

The girl loved to be out of doors, chasing butterflies and plucking wild flowers, far better than sitting at her spinning-wheel. So when her mother saw one after another of Maisie's companions, who were not nearly so pretty as she was, getting rich husbands, she sighed and said:

"Woe's me, child, for methinks no brave wooer will ever pause at our door while they see thee so idle and thoughtless." But Maisie only laughed.

At last her mother grew really angry, and one bright Spring morning she laid down three heads of lint on the table, saying sharply, "I will have no more of this dallying. People will say that it is my blame that no wooer comes to seek thee. I cannot have thee left on my hands to be laughed at, as the idle maid who would not marry. So now thou must work; and if thou hast not these heads of lint spun into seven hanks of thread in three days, I will e'en speak to the Mother at St. Mary's Convent, and thou wilt go there and learn to be a nun."

Now, though Maisie was an idle girl, she had no wish to be shut up in a nunnery; so she tried not to think of the sunshine outside, but sat down soberly with her distaff.

But, alas! she was so little accustomed to work that she made but slow progress; and although she sat at the spinning-wheel all day, and never once went out of doors, she found at night that she had only spun half a hank of yarn.

The next day it was even worse, for her arms ached so much she could only work very slowly. That night she cried herself to sleep; and next morning, seeing that it was quite hopeless to expect to get her task finished, she threw down her distaff in despair, and ran out of doors.

Near the house was a deep dell, through which ran a tiny stream. Maisie loved this dell, the flowers grew so abundantly there.

This morning she ran down to the edge of the stream, and seated herself on a large stone. It was a glorious morning, the hazel trees were newly covered with leaves, and the branches nodded over her head, and showed like delicate tracery against the blue sky. The primroses and sweet-scented violets peeped out from among the grass, and a little water wagtail came and perched on a stone in the middle of the stream, and bobbed up and down, till it seemed as if he were nodding to Maisie, and as if he were trying to say to her, "Never mind, cheer up."

But the poor girl was in no mood that morning to enjoy the flowers and the birds. Instead of watching them, as she generally did, she hid her face in her hands, and wondered what would become of her. She rocked herself to and fro, as she thought how terrible it would be if her mother fulfilled her threat and shut her up in the Convent of St. Mary, with the grave, solemn-faced sisters, who seemed as if they had completely forgotten what it was like to be young, and run about in the sunshine, and laugh, and pick the fresh Spring flowers.

"Oh, I could not do it, I could not do it," she cried at last. "It would kill me to be a nun."

"And who wants to make a pretty wench like thee into a nun?" asked a queer, cracked voice quite close to her.

Maisie jumped up, and stood staring in front of her as if she had been moonstruck. For, just across the stream from where she had been sitting, there was a curious boulder, with a round hole in the middle of it—for all the world like a big apple with the core taken out.

Maisie knew it well; she had often sat upon it, and wondered how the funny hole came to be there.

It was no wonder that she stared, for, seated on this stone, was the queerest little old woman that she had ever seen in her life. Indeed, had it not been for her silver hair, and the white mutch with the big frill that she wore on her head, Maisie would have taken her for a little girl, she wore such a very short skirt, only reaching down to her knees.

Her face, inside the frill of her cap, was round, and her cheeks were rosy, and she had little black eyes, which twinkled merrily as she looked at the startled maiden. On her shoulders was a black and white checked shawl, and on her legs, which she dangled over the edge of the boulder, she wore black silk stockings and the neatest little shoes, with great silver buckles.

In fact, she would have been quite a pretty old lady had it not been for her lips, which were very long and very thick, and made her look quite ugly in spite of her rosy cheeks and black eyes. Maisie stood and looked at her for such a long time in silence that she repeated her question.

"And who wants to make a pretty wench like thee into a nun? More likely that some gallant gentleman should want to make a bride of thee."

"Oh, no," answered Maisie, "my mother says no gentleman would look at me because I cannot spin."

"Nonsense," said the tiny woman. "Spinning is all very well for old folks like me—my lips, as thou seest, are long and ugly because I have spun so much, for I always wet my fingers with them, the easier to draw the thread from the distaff. No, no, take care of thy beauty, child; do not waste it over the spinning-wheel, nor yet in a nunnery."

"If my mother only thought as thou dost," replied the girl sadly; and, encouraged by the old woman's kindly face, she told her the whole story.

"Well," said the old Dame, "I do not like to see pretty girls weep; what if I were able to help thee, and spin the lint for thee?"

Maisie thought that this offer was too good to be true; but her new friend bade her run home and fetch the lint; and I need not tell you that she required no second bidding.

When she returned she handed the bundle to the little lady, and was about to ask her where she should meet her in order to get the thread from her when it was spun, when a sudden noise behind her made her look round.

She saw nothing; but what was her horror and surprise when she turned back again, to find that the old woman had vanished entirely, lint and all.

She rubbed her eyes, and looked all round, but she was

nowhere to be seen. The girl was utterly bewildered. She wondered if she could have been dreaming, but no that could not be, there were her footprints leading up the bank and down again, where she had gone for the lint, and brought it back, and there was the mark of her foot, wet with dew, on a stone in the middle of the stream, where she had stood when she had handed the lint up to the mysterious little stranger.

What was she to do now? What would her mother say when, in addition to not having finished the task that had been given her, she had to confess to having lost the greater part of the lint also? She ran up and down the little dell, hunting amongst the bushes, and peeping into every nook and cranny of the bank where the little old woman might have hidden herself. It was all in vain; and at last, tired out with the search, she sat down on the stone once more, and presently fell fast asleep.

When she awoke it was evening. The sun had set, and the yellow glow on the western horizon was fast giving place to the silvery light of the moon. She was sitting thinking of the curious events of the day, and gazing at the great boulder opposite, when it seemed to her as if a distant murmur of voices came from it.

With one bound she crossed the stream, and clambered on to the stone. She was right.

Someone was talking underneath it, far down in the ground. She put her ear close to the stone, and listened.

The voice of the queer little old woman came up through the hole. "Ho, ho, my pretty little wench little knows that my name is Habetrot."

Full of curiosity, Maisie put her eye to the opening, and the strangest sight that she had ever seen met her gaze. She seemed to be looking through a telescope into a wonderful little valley. The trees there were brighter and greener than any that she had ever seen before and there were beautiful flowers, quite different from the flowers that grew in her country. The little valley was carpeted with the most exquisite moss, and up and down it walked her tiny friend, busily engaged in spinning.

She was not alone, for round her were a circle of other little old women, who were seated on large white stones, and they were all spinning away as fast as they could.

Occasionally one would look up, and then Maisie saw that they all seemed to have the same long, thick lips that her friend had. She really felt very sorry, as they all looked exceedingly kind, and might have been pretty had it not been for this defect.

One of the Spinstresses sat by herself, and was engaged in winding the thread, which the others had spun, into hanks. Maisie did not think that this little lady looked so nice as the others. She was dressed entirely in grey, and had a big hooked nose, and great horn spectacles. She seemed to be called Slantlie Mab, for Maisie heard Habetrot address her by that name, telling her to make haste and tie up all the thread, for it was getting late, and it was time that the young girl had it to carry home to her mother.

Maisie did not quite know what to do, or how she was to get the thread, for she did not like to shout down the hole in case the queer little old woman should be angry at being watched.

However, Habetrot, as she had called herself, suddenly appeared on the path beside her, with the hanks of thread in her hand.

"Oh, thank you, thank you," cried Maisie. "What can I do to show you how thankful I am?"

"Nothing," answered the Fairy. "For I do not work for reward. Only do not tell your mother who span the thread for thee."

It was now late, and Maisie lost no time in running home with the precious thread upon her shoulder. When she walked into the kitchen she found that her mother had gone to bed. She seemed to have had a busy day, for there, hanging up in the wide chimney, in order to dry, were seven large black puddings.

The fire was low, but bright and clear; and the sight of it and the sight of the puddings suggested to Maisie that she was very hungry, and that fried black puddings were very good.

Flinging the thread down on the table, she hastily pulled off her shoes, so as not to make a noise and awake her mother; and, getting down the frying-pan from the wall, she took one of the black puddings from the chimney, and fried it, and ate it.

Still she felt hungry, so she took another, and then another, till they were all gone. Then she crept upstairs to her little bed and fell fast asleep.

Next morning her mother came downstairs before Maisie was awake. In fact, she had not been able to sleep much for thinking of her daughter's careless ways, and had been sorrowfully making up her mind that she must lose no time in speaking to the Abbess of St. Mary's about this idle girl of hers.

What was her surprise to see on the table the seven beautiful hanks of thread, while, on going to the chimney to take down a black pudding to fry for breakfast, she found that every one of them had been eaten. She did not know whether to laugh for joy that her daughter had been so industrious, or to cry for vexation because all her lovely black puddings—which she had expected would last for a week at least—were gone. In her bewilderment she sang out:

> *"My daughter's spun se'en, se'en, se'en,*
> *My daughter's eaten se'en, se'en, se'en,*
> *And all before daylight."*

Now I forgot to tell you that, about half a mile from where the old farmhouse stood, there was a beautiful Castle, where a very rich young nobleman lived. He was both good and brave, as well as rich; and all the mothers who had pretty daughters used to wish that he would come their way, some day, and fall in love with one of them. But he had never done so, and everyone said, "He is too grand to marry any country girl. One day he will go away to London Town and marry a Duke's daughter."

Well, this fine spring morning it chanced that this young nobleman's favourite horse had lost a shoe, and he was so afraid that any of the grooms might ride it along the hard road, and not on the soft grass at the side, that he said that he would take it to the smithy himself.

So it happened that he was riding along by Maisie's garden gate as her mother came into the garden singing these strange lines.

He stopped his horse, and said good-naturedly, "Good day, Madam; and may I ask why you sing such a strange song?"

Maisie's mother made no answer, but turned and walked into the house; and the young nobleman, being very anxious to know what it all meant, hung his bridle over the garden gate, and followed her.

She pointed to the seven hanks of thread lying on the table, and said, "This hath my daughter done before breakfast."

Then the young man asked to see the Maiden who was so industrious, and her mother went and pulled Maisie from behind the door, where she had hidden herself when the stranger came in; for she had come downstairs while her mother was in the garden.

She looked so lovely in her fresh morning gown of blue gingham, with her auburn hair curling softly round her brow, and her face all over blushes at the sight of such a gallant young man, that he quite lost his heart, and fell in love with her on the spot.

"Ah," said he, "my dear mother always told me to try and find a wife who was both pretty and useful, and I have succeeded beyond my expectations. Do not let our marriage, I pray thee, good Dame, be too long deferred."

Maisie's mother was overjoyed, as you may imagine, at this piece of unexpected good fortune, and busied herself in getting everything ready for the wedding; but Maisie herself was a little perplexed.

She was afraid that she would be expected to spin a great deal when she was married and lived at the Castle, and if that were so, her husband was sure to find out that she was not really such a good spinstress as he thought she was.

In her trouble she went down, the night before her wedding, to the great boulder by the stream in the glen, and, climbing up on it, she laid her head against the stone, and called softly down the hole, "Habetrot, dear Habetrot."

The little old woman soon appeared, and, with twinkling

eyes, asked her what was troubling her so much just when she should have been so happy. And Maisie told her.

"Trouble not thy pretty head about that," answered the Fairy, "but come here with thy bridegroom next week, when the moon is full, and I warrant that he will never ask thee to sit at a spinning-wheel again."

Accordingly, after all the wedding festivities were over and the couple had settled down at the Castle, on the appointed evening Maisie suggested to her husband that they should take a walk together in the moonlight.

She was very anxious to see what the little Fairy would do to help her; for that very day he had been showing her all over her new home, and he had pointed out to her the beautiful new spinning-wheel made of ebony, which had belonged to his mother, saying proudly, "To-morrow, little one, I shall bring some lint from the town, and then the maids will see what clever little fingers my wife has."

Maisie had blushed as red as a rose as she bent over the lovely wheel, and then felt quite sick, as she wondered whatever she would do if Habetrot did not help her.

So on this particular evening, after they had walked in the garden, she said that she should like to go down to the little dell and see how the stream looked by moonlight. So to the dell they went.

As soon as they came to the boulder Maisie put her head against it and whispered, "Habetrot, dear Habetrot"; and in an instant the little old woman appeared.

She bowed in a stately way, as if they were both strangers to her, and said, "Welcome, Sir and Madam, to the Spinsters' Dell." And then she tapped on the root of a great oak tree with a tiny wand which she held in her hand, and a green door, which Maisie never remembered having noticed before, flew open, and they followed the Fairy through it into the other valley which Maisie had seen through the hole in the great stone.

All the little old women were sitting on their white chucky stones busy at work, only they seemed far uglier than they had seemed at first; and Maisie noticed that the reason for this was, that, instead of wearing red skirts and white mutches as they had done before, they now wore caps and dresses of dull grey, and instead of looking happy, they all seemed to be trying who could look most miserable, and who could push out their long lips furthest, as they wet their fingers to draw the thread from their distaffs.

"Save us and help us! What a lot of hideous old witches," exclaimed her husband. "Whatever could this funny old woman mean by bringing a pretty child like thee to look at them? Thou wilt dream of them for a week and a day. Just look at their lips"; and, pushing Maisie behind him, he went up to one of them and asked her what had made her mouth grow so ugly.

She tried to tell him, but all the sound that he could hear was something that sounded like SPIN-N-N.

He asked another one, and her answer sounded like this: SPAN-N-N. He tried a third, and hers sounded like SPUN-N-N.

He seized Maisie by the hand and hurried her through the green door. "By my troth," he said, "my mother's spinning-wheel may turn to gold ere I let thee touch it, if this is what spinning leads to. Rather than that thy pretty face should be spoilt, the linen chests at the Castle may get empty, and remain so for ever!"

So it came to pass that Maisie could be out of doors all day wandering about with her husband, and laughing and singing to her heart's content. And whenever there was lint at the Castle to be spun, it was carried down to the big boulder in the dell and left there, and Habetrot and her companions spun it, and there was no more trouble about the matter.

NIPPIT FIT AND CLIPPIT FIT

In a country, far across the sea, there once dwelt a great and mighty Prince. He lived in a grand Castle, which was full of beautiful furniture, and curious and rare ornaments. And among them was a lovely little glass shoe, which would only fit the tiniest foot imaginable.

And as the Prince was looking at it one day, it struck him what a dainty little lady she would need to be who wore such a very small shoe. And, as he liked dainty people, he made up his mind that he would never marry until he found a maiden who could wear the shoe, and that, when he found her, he would ask her to be his wife.

And he called all his Lords and Courtiers to him, and told them of the determination that he had come to, and asked them to help him in his quest.

And after they had taken counsel together they summoned a trusty Knight, and appointed him the Prince's Ambassador; and told him to take the slipper, and mount a fleet-footed horse, and ride up and down the whole of the Kingdom until he found a lady whom it would fit.

So the Ambassador put the little shoe carefully in his pocket and set out on his errand.

He rode, and he rode, and he rode, going to every town and castle that came in his way, and summoning all the ladies to appear before him to try on the shoe. And, as he caused a Proclamation to be made that whoever could wear it should be the Prince's Bride, I need not tell you that all the ladies in the country-side flocked to wherever the Ambassador chanced to be staying, and begged leave to try on the slipper.

But they were all disappointed, for not one of them, try

as she would, could make her foot small enough to go into the Fairy Shoe; and there were many bitter tears shed in secret, when they returned home, by countless fair ladies who prided themselves on the smallness of their feet, and who had set out full of lively expectation that they would be the successful competitors.

At last the Ambassador arrived at a house where a well-to-do Laird had lived. But the Laird was dead now, and there was nobody left but his wife and two daughters, who had grown poor of late, and who had to work hard for their living.

One of the daughters was haughty and insolent; the other was little, and young, and modest, and sweet.

When the Ambassador rode into the courtyard of this house, and, holding out the shoe, asked if there were any fair ladies there who would like to try it on, the elder sister, who always thought a great deal of herself, ran forward, and said that she would do so, while the younger girl just shook her head and went on with her work. "For," said she to herself, "though my feet are so little that they might go into the slipper, what would I do as the wife of a great Prince? Folk would just laugh at me, and say that I was not fit for the position. No, no, I am far better to bide as I am."

So the Ambassador gave the glass shoe to the elder sister, who carried it away to her own room; and presently, to every one's astonishment, came back wearing it on her foot.

It is true that her face was very white, and that she walked with a little limp; but no one noticed these things except her younger sister, and she only shook her wise little head, and said nothing.

The Prince's Ambassador was delighted that he had at last found a wife for his master, and he mounted his horse and rode off at full speed to tell him the good news.

When the Prince heard of the success of his errand, he ordered all his Courtiers to be ready to accompany him next day when he went to bring home his Bride.

You can fancy what excitement there was at the Laird's house when the gallant company arrived, with their Prince at their head, to greet the lady who was to be their Princess.

The old mother and the plain-looking maid-of-all-work ran hither and thither, fetching such meat and drink as the house could boast to set before their high-born visitors, while the bonnie little sister went and hid herself behind a great pot which stood in the corner of the courtyard, and which was used for boiling hen's meat.

She knew that her foot was the smallest in the house; and something told her that if the Prince once got a glimpse of her he would not be content till she had tried on the slipper.

Meanwhile, the selfish elder sister did not help at all, but ran up to her chamber, and decked herself out in all the fine clothes that she possessed before she came downstairs to meet the Prince.

And when all the Knights and Courtiers had drunk a stir-rup-cup, and wished Good Luck to their Lord and his Bride, she was lifted up behind the Prince on his horse, and rode off so full of her own importance, that she even forgot to say good-bye to her mother and sister.

Alas! alas! pride must have a fall. For the cavalcade had not proceeded very far when a little bird which was perched on a branch of a bush by the roadside sang out:

"Nippit fit, and clippit fit, behind the King rides, But pretty fit, and little fit, ahint the caldron hides."

"What is this that the birdie says?" cried the Prince, who,

if the truth be told, did not feel altogether satisfied with the Bride whom fortune had bestowed upon him. "Hast thou another sister, Madam?"

"Only a little one," murmured the lady, who liked ill the way in which things seemed to be falling out.

"We will go back and find her," said the Prince firmly, "for when I sent out the slipper I had no mind that its wearer should nip her foot, and clip her foot, in order to get it on."

So the whole party turned back; and when they reached the Laird's house the Prince ordered a search to be made in the courtyard. And the bonnie little sister was soon discovered and brought out, all blushes and confusion, from her hiding-place behind the caldron.

"Give her the slipper, and let her try it on," said the Prince, and the eldest sister was forced to obey. And what was the horror of the bystanders, as she drew it off, to see that she had cut off the tops of her toes in order to get it on.

But it fitted her little sister's foot exactly, without either paring or clipping; and when the Prince saw that it was so, he lifted the elder sister down from his horse and lifted the little one up in her place, and carried her home to his Palace, where the wedding was celebrated with great rejoicing; and for the rest of their lives they were the happiest couple in the whole kingdom.

THE FAIRIES OF
MERLIN'S CRAG

About two hundred years ago there was a poor man working as a labourer on a farm in Lanarkshire. He was what is known as an "Orra Man"; that is, he had no special work mapped out for him to do, but he was expected to undertake odd jobs of any kind that happened to turn up.

One day his master sent him out to cast peats on a piece of moorland that lay on a certain part of the farm. Now this strip of moorland ran up at one end to a curiously shaped crag, known as Merlin's Crag, because, so the country folk said, that famous Enchanter had once taken up his abode there.

The man obeyed, and, being a willing fellow, when he arrived at the moor he set to work with all his might and main. He had lifted quite a quantity of peat from near the Crag, when he was startled by the appearance of the very smallest woman that he had ever seen in his life. She was only about two feet high, and she was dressed in a green gown and red stockings, and her long yellow hair was not bound by any ribbon, but hung loosely round her shoulders.

She was such a dainty little creature that the astonished countryman stopped working, stuck his spade into the ground, and gazed at her in wonder.

His wonder increased when she held up one of her tiny fingers and addressed him in these words: "What wouldst thou think if I were to send my husband to uncover thy house? You mortals think that you can do aught that pleaseth you."

Then, stamping her tiny foot, she added in a voice of command, "Put back that turf instantly, or thou shalt rue this day."

Now the poor man had often heard of the Fairy Folk and of the harm that they could work to unthinking mortals who offended them, so in fear and trembling he set to work to undo all his labour, and to place every divot in the exact spot from which he had taken it.

When he was finished he looked round for his strange visitor, but she had vanished completely; he could not tell how, nor where. Putting up his spade, he wended his way homewards, and going straight to his master, he told him the whole story, and suggested that in future the peats should be taken from the other end of the moor.

But the master only laughed. He was a strong, hearty man, and had no belief in Ghosts, or Elves, or Fairies, or any other creature that he could not see; but although he laughed, he was vexed that his servant should believe in such things, so to cure him, as he thought, of his superstition, he ordered him to take a horse and cart and go back at once, and lift all the peats and bring them to dry in the farm steading.

The poor man obeyed with much reluctance; and was greatly relieved, as weeks went on, to find that, in spite of his having done so, no harm befell him.

In fact, he began to think that his master was right, and that the whole thing must have been a dream.

So matters went smoothly on. Winter passed, and spring, and summer, until autumn came round once more, and the very day arrived on which the peats had been lifted the year before.

That day, as the sun went down, the orra man left the farm to go home to his cottage, and as his master was pleased with him because he had been working very hard lately, he had given him a little can of milk as a present to carry home to his wife.

So he was feeling very happy, and as he walked along he was humming a tune to himself. His road took him by the foot of Merlin's Crag, and as he approached it he was astonished to find himself growing strangely tired. His eyelids dropped over his eyes as if he were going to sleep, and his feet grew as heavy as lead.

"I will sit down and take a rest for a few minutes," he said to himself; "the road home never seemed so long as it does to-day."

So he sat down on a tuft of grass right under the shadow of the Crag, and before he knew where he was he had fallen into a deep and heavy slumber.

When he awoke it was near midnight, and the moon had risen on the Crag. And he rubbed his eyes, when by its soft light he became aware of a large band of Fairies who were dancing round and round him, singing and laughing, pointing their tiny fingers at him, and shaking their wee fists in his face.

The bewildered man rose and tried to walk away from them, but turn in whichever direction he would the Fairies accompanied him, encircling him in a magic ring, out of which he could in no wise go.

At last they stopped, and, with shrieks of elfin laughter, led the prettiest and daintiest of their companions up to him, and cried, "Tread a measure, tread a measure, Oh, Man! Then wilt thou not be so eager to escape from our company."

Now the poor labourer was but a clumsy dancer, and he held back with a shamefaced air; but the Fairy who had been chosen to be his partner reached up and seized his hands, and lo! some strange magic seemed to enter into his veins, for in a moment he found himself waltzing and whirling, sliding and bowing, as if he had done nothing else but dance all his life.

And, strangest thing of all! he forgot about his home and his children; and he felt so happy that he had no longer the slightest desire to leave the Fairies' company.

All night long the merriment went on. The Little Folk danced and danced as if they were mad, and the farm man danced with them, until at last a shrill sound came over the moor. It was the cock from the farmyard crowing its loudest to welcome the dawn.

In an instant the revelry ceased, and the Fairies, with cries of alarm, crowded together and rushed towards the Crag, dragging the countryman along in their midst. As they reached the rock, a mysterious door, which he never remembered having seen before, opened in it of its own accord, and shut again with a crash as soon as the Fairy Host had all trooped through.

The door led into a large, dimly lighted hall full of tiny couches, and here the Little Folk sank to rest, tired out with their exertions, while the good man sat down on a piece of rock in the corner, wondering what would happen next.

But there seemed to be some kind of spell thrown over his senses, for even when the Fairies awoke and began to go about their household occupations, and to carry out certain curious practices which he had never seen before, and which, as you will hear, he was forbidden to speak of afterwards, he was content to sit and watch them, without in any way attempting to escape.

As it drew toward evening someone touched his elbow, and he turned round with a start to see the little woman with the green dress and scarlet stockings, who had remonstrated with him for lifting the turf the year before, standing by his side.

"The divots which thou took'st from the roof of my house have grown once more," she said, "and once more it is covered with grass; so thou canst go home again, for justice is satisfied—thy punishment hath lasted long enough. But first must thou take thy solemn oath never to tell to mortal ears what thou hast seen whilst thou hast dwelt among us."

The countryman promised gladly, and took the oath with all due solemnity. Then the door was opened, and he was at liberty to depart.

His can of milk was standing on the green, just where he had laid it down when he went to sleep; and it seemed to him as if it were only yesternight that the farmer had given it to him.

But when he reached his home he was speedily undeceived. For his wife looked at him as if he were a ghost, and the children whom he had left wee, toddling things were now well-grown boys and girls, who stared at him as if he had been an utter stranger.

"Where hast thou been these long, long years?" cried his wife when she had gathered her wits and seen that it was really he, and not a spirit. "And how couldst thou find it in thy heart to leave the bairns and me alone?"

And then he knew that the one day he had passed in Fairy-land had lasted seven whole years, and he realised how heavy the punishment had been which the Wee Folk had laid upon him.

THE WEDDING OF ROBIN REDBREAST AND JENNY WREN

There was once an old grey Pussy Baudrons, and she went out for a stroll one Christmas morning to see what she could see. And as she was walking down the burnside she saw a little Robin Redbreast hopping up and down on the branches of a briar bush.

"What a tasty breakfast he would make," thought she to herself. "I must try to catch him."

So, "Good morning, Robin Redbreast," quoth she, sitting down on her tail at the foot of the briar bush and looking up at him. "And where mayest thou be going so early on this cold winter's day?"

"I'm on my road to the King's Palace," answered Robin cheerily, "to sing him a song this merry Yule morning."

"That's a pious errand to be travelling on, and I wish you good success," replied Pussy slyly; "but just hop down a minute before thou goest, and I will show thee what a bonnie white ring I have round my neck. 'Tis few cats that are marked like me."

Then Robin cocked his head on one side, and looked down on Pussy Baudrons with a twinkle in his eye. "Ha, ha! grey Pussy Baudrons," he said. "Ha, ha! for I saw thee worry the little grey mouse, and I have no wish that thou shouldst worry me."

And with that he spread his wings and flew away. And he flew, and he flew, till he lighted on an old sod dyke; and there he saw a greedy old gled sitting, with all his feathers ruffled up as if he felt cold.

"Good morning, Robin Redbreast," cried the greedy old gled, who had had no food since yesterday, and was therefore very hungry. "And where mayest thou be going to, this cold winter's day?"

"I'm on my road to the King's Palace," answered Robin, "to sing to him a song this merry Yule morning." And he hopped away a yard or two from the gled, for there was a look in his eye that he did not quite like.

"Thou art a friendly little fellow," remarked the gled sweetly, "and I wish thee good luck on thine errand; but ere thou go on, come nearer me, I prith'ee, and I will show thee what a curious feather I have in my wing. 'Tis said that no other gled in the country-side hath one like it."

"Like enough," rejoined Robin, hopping still further away; "but I will take thy word for it, without seeing it. For I saw thee pluck the feathers from the wee lintie, and I have no wish that thou shouldst pluck the feathers from me. So I will bid thee good day, and go on my journey."

The next place on which he rested was a piece of rock that overhung a dark, deep glen, and here he saw a sly old fox looking out of his hole not two yards below him.

"Good morning, Robin Redbreast," said the sly old fox, who had tried to steal a fat duck from a farmyard the night before, and had barely escaped with his life. "And where mayest thou be going so early on this cold winter's day?"

"I'm on my road to the King's Palace, to sing him a song this merry Yule morning," answered Robin, giving the same answer that he had given to the grey Pussy Baudrons and the greedy gled.

"Thou wilt get a right good welcome, for His Majesty is fond of music," said the wily fox. "But ere thou go, just come down and have a look at a black spot which I have on the end of my tail. 'Tis said that there is not a fox 'twixt here and the Border that hath a spot on his tail like mine."

"Very like, very like," replied Robin; "but I chanced to see thee worrying the wee lambie up on the braeside yonder, and I have no wish that thou shouldst try thy teeth on me. So I will e'en go on my way to the King's Palace, and thou canst show the spot on thy tail to the next passer-by."

So the little Robin Redbreast flew away once more, and never rested till he came to a bonnie valley with a little burn running through it, and there he saw a rosy-cheeked boy sitting on a log eating a piece of bread and butter. And he perched on a branch and watched him.

"Good morning, Robin Redbreast; and where mayest thou be going so early on this cold winter's day?" asked the boy eagerly; for he was making a collection of stuffed birds, and he had still to get a Robin Redbreast.

"I'm on my way to the King's Palace to sing him a song this merry Yule morning," answered Robin, hopping down to the ground, and keeping one eye fixed on the bread and butter.

"Come a bit nearer, Robin," said the boy, "and I will give thee some crumbs."

"Na, na, my wee man," chirped the cautious little bird; "for I saw thee catch the goldfinch, and I have no wish to give thee the chance to catch me."

At last he came to the King's Palace and lighted on the window-sill, and there he sat and sang the very sweetest song that he could sing; for he felt so happy because it was the Blessed Yuletide, that he wanted everyone else to be happy too. And the King and the Queen were so delighted with his song, as he peeped in at them at their open window, that they asked each other what they could give him as a reward for his kind thought in coming so far to greet them.

"We can give him a wife," replied the Queen, "who will go home with him and help him to build his nest."

"And who wilt thou give him for a bride?" asked the King. "Methinks 'twould need to be a very tiny lady to match his size."

"Why, Jenny Wren, of course," answered the Queen. "She hath looked somewhat dowie of late, this will be the very thing to brighten her up."

Then the King clapped his hands, and praised his wife for her happy thought, and wondered that the idea had not struck him before.

So Robin Redbreast and Jenny Wren were married, amid great rejoicings, at the King's Palace; and the King and Queen and all the fine Nobles and Court Ladies danced at their wedding. Then they flew away home to Robin's own country-side, and built their nest in the roots of the briar bush, where he had spoken to Pussie Baudrons. And you will be glad to hear that Jenny Wren proved the best little housewife in the world.

THE DWARFIE STONE

Far up in a green valley in the Island of Hoy stands an immense boulder. It is hollow inside, and the natives of these northern islands call it the Dwarfie Stone, because long centuries ago, so the legend has it, Snorro the Dwarf lived there.

Nobody knew where Snorro came from, or how long he had dwelt in the dark chamber inside the Dwarfie Stone. All that they knew about him was that he was a little man, with a queer, twisted, deformed body and a face of marvellous beauty, which never seemed to look any older, but was always smiling and young.

Men said that this was because Snorro's father had been a Fairy, and not a denizen of earth, who had bequeathed to his son the gift of perpetual youth, but nobody knew whether this were true or not, for the Dwarf had inhabited the Dwarfie Stone long before the oldest man or woman in Hoy had been born.

One thing was certain, however: he had inherited from his mother, whom all men agreed had been mortal, the dangerous qualities of vanity and ambition. And the longer he lived the more vain and ambitious did he become, until at last he always carried a mirror of polished steel round his neck, into which he constantly looked in order to see the reflection of his handsome face.

And he would not attend to the country people who came to seek his help, unless they bowed themselves humbly before him and spoke to him as if he were a King.

I say that the country people sought his help, for he spent his time, or appeared to spend it, in collecting herbs and simples on the hillsides, which he carried home with him to his dark abode, and distilled medicines and potions from them, which he sold to his neighbours at wondrous high prices.

He was also the possessor of a wonderful leathern-covered book, clasped with clasps of brass, over which he would pore for hours together, and out of which he would tell the simple Islanders their fortunes, if they would.

For they feared the book almost as much as they feared Snorro himself, for it was whispered that it had once belonged to Odin, and they crossed themselves for protection as they named the mighty Enchanter.

But all the time they never guessed the real reason why Snorro chose to live in the Dwarfie Stone.

I will tell you why he did so. Not very far from the Stone there was a curious hill, shaped exactly like a wart. It was known as the Wart Hill of Hoy, and men said that somewhere in the side of it was hidden a wonderful carbuncle, which, when it was found, would bestow on its finder marvellous magic gifts—Health, Wealth, and Happiness. Everything, in fact, that a human being could desire.

And the curious thing about this carbuncle was, that it was said that it could be seen at certain times, if only the people who were looking for it were at the right spot at the right moment.

Now Snorro had made up his mind that he would find this wonderful stone, so, while he pretended to spend all his time in reading his great book or distilling medicines from his herbs, he was really keeping a keen look-out during his wanderings, noting every tuft of grass or piece of rock under which it might be hidden. And at night, when everyone else was asleep, he would creep out, with pickaxe and spade, to turn over the rocks or dig over the turf, in the hope of finding the long-sought-for treasure underneath them.

He was always accompanied on these occasions by an enormous grey-headed Raven, who lived in the cave along with him, and who was his bosom friend and companion. The Islanders feared this bird of ill omen as much, perhaps, as they feared its Master; for, although they went to consult Snorro in all their difficulties and perplexities, and bought medicines and love-potions from him, they always looked upon him with a certain dread, feeling that there was something weird and uncanny about him.

Now, at the time we are speaking of, Orkney was governed by two Earls, who were half-brothers. Paul, the elder, was a tall, handsome man, with dark hair, and eyes like sloes. All the country people loved him, for he was so skilled in knightly exercises, and had such a sweet and loving nature, that no one could help being fond of him. Old people's eyes would brighten at the sight of him, and the little children would run out to greet him as he rode by their mothers' doors.

And this was the more remarkable because, with all his winning manner, he had such a lack of conversation that men called him Paul the Silent, or Paul the Taciturn.

Harold, on the other hand, was as different from his brother as night is from day. He was fair-haired and blue-eyed, and he had gained for himself the name of Harold the Orator, because he was always free of speech and ready with his tongue.

But for all this he was not a favourite. For he was haughty, and jealous, and quick-tempered, and the old folks' eyes did not brighten at the sight of him, and the babes, instead of toddling out to greet him, hid their faces in their mothers' skirts when they saw him coming.

Harold could not help knowing that the people liked his silent brother best, and the knowledge made him jealous of him, so a coldness sprang up between them.

Now it chanced, one summer, that Earl Harold went on a visit to the King of Scotland, accompanied by his mother, the Countess Helga, and her sister, the Countess Fraukirk.

And while he was at Court he met a charming young Irish lady, the Lady Morna, who had come from Ireland to Scotland to attend upon the Scottish Queen. She was so sweet, and good, and gentle that Earl Harold's heart was won, and he made up his mind that she, and only she, should be his bride.

But although he had paid her much attention, Lady Morna had sometimes caught glimpses of his jealous temper; she had seen an evil expression in his eyes, and had heard him speak sharply to his servants, and she had no wish to marry him. So, to his great amazement, she refused the honour which he offered her, and told him that she would prefer to remain as she was.

Earl Harold ground his teeth in silent rage, but he saw that it was no use pressing his suit at that moment. So what he could not obtain by his own merits he determined to obtain by guile.

Accordingly he begged his mother to persuade the Lady Morna to go back with them on a visit, hoping that when she was alone with him in Orkney, he would be able to overcome her prejudice against him, and induce her to become his wife. And all the while he never remembered his brother Paul; or, if he did, he never thought it possible that he could be his rival.

But that was just the very thing that happened. The Lady Morna, thinking no evil, accepted the Countess Helga's invitation, and no sooner had the party arrived back in Orkney than Paul, charmed with the grace and beauty of the fair Irish Maiden, fell head over ears in love with her. And the Lady Morna, from the very first hour that she saw him, returned his love.

Of course this state of things could not long go on hidden, and when Harold realised what had happened his anger and jealousy knew no bounds. Seizing a dagger, he rushed up to the turret where his brother was sitting in his private apartments, and threatened to stab him to the heart if he did not promise to give up all thoughts of winning the lovely stranger.

But Paul met him with pleasant words.

"Calm thyself, Brother," he said. "It is true that I love the lady, but that is no proof that I shall win her. Is it likely that she will choose me, whom all men name Paul the Silent, when she hath the chance of marrying you, whose tongue moves so swiftly that to you is given the proud title of Harold the Orator?"

At these words Harold's vanity was flattered, and he thought that, after all, his step-brother was right, and that he had a very small chance, with his meagre gift of speech, of being successful in his suit. So he threw down his dagger, and, shaking hands with him, begged him to pardon his unkind thoughts, and went down the winding stair again in high good-humour with himself and all the world.

By this time it was coming near to the Feast of Yule, and at that Festival it was the custom for the Earl and his Court to leave Kirkwall for some weeks, and go to the great Palace of Orphir, nine miles distant. And in order to see that everything was ready, Earl Paul took his departure some days before the others.

The evening before he left he chanced to find the Lady

Morna sitting alone in one of the deep windows of the great hall. She had been weeping, for she was full of sadness at the thought of his departure; and at the sight of her distress the kind-hearted young Earl could no longer contain himself, but, folding her in his arms, he whispered to her how much he loved her, and begged her to promise to be his wife.

She agreed willingly. Hiding her rosy face on his shoulder, she confessed that she had loved him from the very first day that she had seen him; and ever since that moment she had determined that, if she could not wed him, she would wed no other man.

For a little time they sat together, rejoicing in their new-found happiness. Then Earl Paul sprang to his feet.

"Let us go and tell the good news to my mother and my brother," he said. "Harold may be disappointed at first, for I know, Sweetheart, he would fain have had thee for his own. But his good heart will soon overcome all that, and he will rejoice with us also."

But the Lady Morna shook her head. She knew, better than her lover, what Earl Harold's feeling would be; and she would fain put off the evil hour.

"Let us hold our peace till after Yule," she pleaded. "It will be a joy to keep our secret to ourselves for a little space; there will be time enough then to let all the world know."

Rather reluctantly, Earl Paul agreed; and next day he set off for the Palace at Orphir, leaving his lady-love behind him.

Little he guessed the danger he was in! For, all unknown to him, his step-aunt, Countess Fraukirk, had chanced to be in the hall, the evening before, hidden behind a curtain, and she had overheard every word that Morna and he had spoken, and her heart was filled with black rage.

For she was a hard, ambitious woman, and she had always hated the young Earl, who was no blood-relation to her, and who stood in the way of his brother, her own nephew; for, if Paul were only dead, Harold would be the sole Earl of Orkney.

And now that he had stolen the heart of the Lady Morna, whom her own nephew loved, her hate and anger knew no bounds. She had hastened off to her sister's chamber as soon as the lovers had parted; and there the two women had remained talking together till the chilly dawn broke in the sky.

Next day a boat went speeding over the narrow channel of water that separates Pomona (on the mainland) from Hoy. In it sat a woman, but who she was, or what she was like, no one could say, for she was covered from head to foot with a black cloak, and her face was hidden behind a thick, dark veil.

Snorro the Dwarf knew her, even before she laid aside her trappings, for Countess Fraukirk was no stranger to him. In the course of her long life she had often had occasion to seek his aid to help her in her evil deeds, and she had always paid him well for his services in yellow gold. He therefore welcomed her gladly; but when he had heard the nature of her errand his smiling face grew grave again, and he shook his head.

"I have served thee well, Lady, in the past," he said, "but methinks that this thing goeth beyond my courage. For to compass an Earl's death is a weighty matter, especially when he is so well beloved as is the Earl Paul.

"Thou knowest why I have taken up my abode in this lonely spot—how I hope some day to light upon the magic carbuncle. Thou knowest also how the people fear me, and hate me too, forsooth. And if the young Earl died, and suspicion fell on me, I must needs fly the Island, for my life would not be worth a grain of sand. Then my chance of success would be gone. Nay! I cannot do it, Lady; I cannot do it."

But the wily Countess offered him much gold, and bribed him higher and higher, first with wealth, then with success, and lastly she promised to obtain for him a high post at the Court of the King of Scotland; and at that his ambition stirred within him, his determination gave way, and he consented to do what she asked.

"I will summon my magic loom," he said, "and weave a piece of cloth of finest texture and of marvellous beauty; and before I weave it I will so poison the thread with a magic potion that, when it is fashioned into a garment, whoever puts it on will die ere he hath worn it many minutes."

"Thou art a clever knave," answered the Countess, a cruel smile lighting up her evil face, "and thou shalt be rewarded. Let me have a couple of yards of this wonderful web, and I will make a bonnie waistcoat for my fine young Earl and give it to him as a Yuletide gift. Then I reckon that he will not see the year out."

"That will he not," said Dwarf Snorro, with a malicious grin; and the two parted, after arranging that the piece of cloth should be delivered at the Palace of Orphir on the day before Christmas Eve.

Now, when the Countess Fraukirk had been away upon her wicked errand, strange things were happening at the Castle at Kirkwall. For Harold, encouraged by his brother's absence, offered his heart and hand once more to the Lady Morna. Once more she refused him, and in order to make sure that the scene should not be repeated, she told him that she had plighted her troth to his brother. When he heard that this was so, rage and fury were like to devour him. Mad with anger, he rushed from her presence, flung himself upon his horse, and rode away in the direction of the sea shore.

While he was galloping wildly along, his eyes fell on the snow-clad hills of Hoy rising up across the strip of sea that divided the one island from the other. And his thoughts flew at once to Snorro the Dwarf, who he had had occasion, as well as his step-aunt, to visit in bygone days.

"I have it," he cried. "Stupid fool that I was not to think of it at once. I will go to Snorro, and buy from him a love-potion, which will make my Lady Morna hate my precious brother and turn her thoughts kindly towards me."

So he made haste to hire a boat, and soon he was speeding over the tossing waters on his way to the Island of Hoy. When he arrived there he hurried up the lonely valley to where the Dwarfie Stone stood, and he had no difficulty in finding its uncanny occupant, for Snorro was standing at the hole that served as a door, his raven on his shoulder, gazing placidly at the setting sun.

A curious smile crossed his face when, hearing the sound of approaching footsteps, he turned round and his eyes fell on the young noble.

"What bringeth thee here, Sir Earl?" he asked gaily, for he scented more gold.

"I come for a love-potion," said Harold; and without more ado he told the whole story to the Wizard. "I will pay thee for it," he added, "if thou wilt give it to me quickly."

Snorro looked at him from head to foot. "Blind must the maiden be, Sir Orator," he said, "who needeth a love-potion to make her fancy so gallant a Knight."

Earl Harold laughed angrily. "It is easier to catch a sunbeam than a woman's roving fancy," he replied. "I have no time for jesting. For, hearken, old man, there is a proverb that saith, 'Time and tide wait for no man,' so I need not expect the tide to wait for me. The potion I must have, and that instantly."

Snorro saw that he was in earnest, so without a word he entered his dwelling, and in a few minutes returned with a small phial in his hand, which was full of a rosy liquid.

"Pour the contents of this into the Lady Morna's wine-cup," he said, "and I warrant thee that before four-and-twenty hours have passed she will love thee better than thou lovest her now."

Then he waved his hand, as if to dismiss his visitor, and disappeared into his dwelling-place.

Earl Harold made all speed back to the Castle; but it was not until one or two days had elapsed that he found a chance to pour the love-potion into the Lady Morna's wine-cup. But at last, one night at supper, he found an opportunity of doing so, and, waving away the little page-boy, he handed it to her himself.

She raised it to her lips, but she only made a pretence at drinking, for she had seen the hated Earl fingering the cup, and she feared some deed of treachery. When he had gone back to his seat she managed to pour the whole of the wine on the floor, and smiled to herself at the look of satisfaction that came over Harold's face as she put down the empty cup.

His satisfaction increased, for from that moment she felt so afraid of him that she treated him with great kindness, hoping that by doing so she would keep in his good graces until the Court moved to Orphir, and her own true love could protect her.

Harold, on his side, was delighted with her graciousness,

for he felt certain that the charm was beginning to work, and that his hopes would soon be fulfilled.

A week later the Court removed to the Royal Palace at Orphir, where Earl Paul had everything in readiness for the reception of his guests.

Of course he was overjoyed to meet Lady Morna again, and she was overjoyed to meet him, for she felt that she was now safe from the unwelcome attentions of Earl Harold.

But to Earl Harold the sight of their joy was as gall and bitterness, and he could scarcely contain himself, although he still trusted in the efficacy of Snorro the Dwarf's love-potion.

As for Countess Fraukirk and Countess Helga, they looked forward eagerly to the time when the magic web would arrive, out of which they hoped to fashion a fatal gift for Earl Paul.

At last, the day before Christmas Eve, the two wicked women were sitting in the Countess Helga's chamber talking of the time when Earl Harold would rule alone in Orkney, when a tap came to the window, and on looking round they saw Dwarf Snorro's grey-headed Raven perched on the sill, a sealed packet in its beak.

They opened the casement, and with a hoarse croak the creature let the packet drop on to the floor; then it flapped its great wings and rose slowly into the air again its head turned in the direction of Hoy.

With fingers that trembled with excitement they broke the seals and undid the packet. It contained a piece of the most beautiful material that anyone could possibly imagine, woven in all the colours of the rainbow, and sparkling with gold and jewels.

"'Twill make a bonnie waistcoat," exclaimed Countess

Fraukirk, with an unholy laugh. "The Silent Earl will be a braw man when he gets it on."

Then, without more ado, they set to work to cut out and sew the garment. All that night they worked, and all next day, till, late in the afternoon, when they were putting in the last stitches, hurried footsteps were heard ascending the winding staircase, and Earl Harold burst open the door.

His cheeks were red with passion, and his eyes were bright, for he could not but notice that, now that she was safe at Orphir under her true love's protection, the Lady Morna's manner had grown cold and distant again, and he was beginning to lose faith in Snorro's charm.

Angry and disappointed, he had sought his mother's room to pour out his story of vexation to her.

He stopped short, however, when he saw the wonderful waistcoat lying on the table, all gold and silver and shining colours. It was like a fairy garment, and its beauty took his breath away.

"For whom hast thou purchased that?" he asked, hoping to hear that it was intended for him.

"'Tis a Christmas gift for thy brother Paul," answered his mother, and she would have gone on to tell him how deadly a thing it was, had he given her time to speak. But her words fanned his fury into madness, for it seemed to him that this hated brother of his was claiming everything.

"Everything is for Paul! I am sick of his very name," he cried. "By my troth, he shall not have this!" and he snatched the vest from the table.

It was in vain that his mother and his aunt threw themselves at his feet, begging him to lay it down, and warning him that there was not a thread in it which was not poisoned. He paid no heed to their words, but rushed from the room, and, drawing it on, ran downstairs with a reckless laugh, to show the Lady Morna how fine he was.

Alas! alas! Scarce had he gained the hall than he fell to the ground in great pain.

Everyone crowded round him, and the two Countesses, terrified now by what they had done, tried in vain to tear the magic vest from his body. But he felt that it was too late, the deadly poison had done its work, and, waving them aside, he turned to his brother, who, in great distress, had knelt down and taken him tenderly in his arms.

"I wronged thee, Paul," he gasped. "For thou hast ever been true and kind. Forgive me in thy thoughts, and," he added, gathering up his strength for one last effort, and pointing to the two wretched women who had wrought all this misery, "*Beware of those two women*, for they seek to take thy life." Then his head sank back on his brother's shoulder, and, with one long sigh, he died.

When he learned what had happened, and understood where the waistcoat came from, and for what purpose it had been intended, the anger of the Silent Earl knew no bounds. He swore a great oath that he would be avenged, not only on Snorro the Dwarf, but also on his wicked step-mother and her cruel sister.

His vengeance was baulked, however, for in the panic and confusion that followed Harold's death, the two Countesses slipped out of the Palace and fled to the coast, and took boat in haste to Scotland, where they had great possessions, and where they were much looked up to, and where no one would believe a word against them.

But retribution fell on them in the end, as it always does

fall, sooner or later, on everyone who is wicked, or selfish, or cruel; for the Norsemen invaded the land, and their Castle was set on fire, and they perished miserably in the flames.

When Earl Paul found that they had escaped, he set out in hot haste for the Island of Hoy, for he was determined that the Dwarf, at least, should not escape. But when he came to the Dwarfie Stone he found it silent and deserted, all trace of its uncanny occupants having disappeared.

No one knew what had become of them; a few people were inclined to think that the Dwarf and his Raven had accompanied the Countess Fraukirk and the Countess Helga on their flight, but the greater part of the Islanders held to the belief, which I think was the true one, that the Powers of the Air spirited Snorro away, and shut him up in some unknown place as a punishment for his wickedness, and that his Raven accompanied him.

At any rate, he was never seen again by any living person, and wherever he went, he lost all chance of finding the magic carbuncle.

As for the Silent Earl and his Irish Sweetheart, they were married as soon as Earl Harold's funeral was over; and for hundreds of years afterwards, when the inhabitants of the Orkney Isles wanted to express great happiness, they said, "As happy as Earl Paul and the Countess Morna."

CANONBIE DICK AND THOMAS OF ERCILDOUNE

It chanced, long years ago, that a certain horse-dealer lived in the South of Scotland, near the Border, not very far from Longtown. He was known as Canonbie Dick; and as he went up and down the country, he almost always had a long string of horses behind him, which he bought at one fair and sold at another, generally managing to turn a good big penny by the transaction.

He was a very fearless man, not easily daunted; and the people who knew him used to say that if Canonbie Dick dare not attempt a thing, no one else need be asked to do it.

One evening, as he was returning from a fair at some distance from his home with a pair of horses which he had not succeeded in selling, he was riding over Bowden Moor, which lies to the west of the Eildon Hills. These hills are, as all men know, the scene of some of the most famous of Thomas the Rhymer's prophecies; and also, so men say, they are the sleeping-place of King Arthur and his Knights, who rest under the three high peaks, waiting for the mystic call that shall awake them.

But little recked the horse-dealer of Arthur and his Knights, nor yet of Thomas the Rhymer. He was riding along at a snail's pace, thinking over the bargains which he had made at the fair that day, and wondering when he was likely to dispose of his two remaining horses.

All at once he was startled by the approach of a venerable man, with white hair and an old-world dress, who seemed almost to start out of the ground, so suddenly did he make his appearance.

When they met, the stranger stopped, and, to Canonbie Dick's great amazement, asked him for how much he would be willing to part with his horses.

The wily horse-dealer thought that he saw a chance of driving a good bargain, for the stranger looked a man of some consequence; so he named a good round sum.

The old man tried to bargain with him; but when he found that he had not much chance of succeeding—for no one ever did succeed in inducing Canonbie Dick to sell a horse for a less sum than he named for it at first—he agreed to buy the animals, and, pulling a bag of gold from the pocket of his queerly cut breeches, he began to count out the price.

As he did so, Canonbie Dick got another shock of surprise, for the gold that the stranger gave him was not the gold that was in use at the time, but was fashioned into Unicorns, and Bonnet-pieces, and other ancient coins, which would be of no use to the horse-dealer in his everyday transactions. But it was good, pure gold; and he took it gladly, for he knew that he was selling his horses at about half as much again as they were worth. "So," thought he to himself, "surely I cannot be the loser in the long run."

Then the two parted, but not before the old man had commissioned Dick to get him other good horses at the same price, the only stipulation he made being that Dick should always bring them to the same spot, after dark, and that he should always come alone.

And, as time went on, the horse-dealer found that he had indeed met a good customer.

For, whenever he came across a suitable horse, he had only to lead it over Bowden Moor after dark, and he was sure to meet the mysterious, white-headed stranger, who always paid him for the animal in old-fashioned golden pieces.

And he might have been selling horses to him yet, for aught I know, had it not been for his one failing.

Canonbie Dick was apt to get very thirsty, and his ordinary customers, knowing this, took care always to provide him with something to drink. The old man never did so; he paid down his money and led away his horses, and there was an end of the matter.

But one night, Dick, being even more thirsty than usual, and feeling sure that his mysterious friend must live somewhere in the neighbourhood, seeing that he was always wandering about the hillside when everyone else was asleep, hinted that he would be very glad to go home with him and have a little refreshment.

"He would need to be a brave man who asks to go home with me," returned the stranger; "but, if thou wilt, thou canst follow me. Only, remember this—if thy courage fail thee at that which thou wilt behold, thou wilt rue it all thy life."

Canonbie Dick laughed long and loud. "My courage hath never failed me yet," he cried. "Beshrew me if I will let it fail now. So lead on, old man, and I will follow."

Without a word the stranger turned and began to ascend a narrow path which led to a curious hillock, which from its shape, was called by the country-folk the "Lucken Hare."

It was supposed to be a great haunt of Witches; and, as a rule, nobody passed that way after dark, if they could possibly help it.

Canonbie Dick was not afraid of Witches, however, so he followed his guide with a bold step up the hillside; but it must be confessed that he felt a little startled when he saw him turn down what seemed to be an entrance to a cavern, especially as he never remembered having seen any opening in the hillside there before.

He paused for a moment, looking round him in perplexity, wondering where he was being taken; and his conductor glanced at him scornfully.

"You can go back if you will," he said. "I warned thee thou wert going on a journey that would try thy courage to the uttermost." There was a jeering note in his voice that touched Dick's pride.

"Who said that I was afraid?" he retorted. "I was just taking note of where this passage stands on the hillside, so as to know it another time."

The stranger shrugged his shoulders. "Time enough to look for it when thou wouldst visit it again," he said. And then he pursued his way, with Dick following closely at his heels.

After the first yard or two they were enveloped in thick darkness, and the horse-dealer would have been sore put to it to keep near his guide had not the latter held out his hand for him to grasp. But after a little space a faint glimmering of light began to appear, which grew clearer and clearer, until at last they found themselves in an enormous cavern lit by flaming torches, which were stuck here and there in sconces in the rocky walls, and which, although they served to give light enough to see by, yet threw such ghostly shadows on the floor that they only seemed to intensify the gloom that hung over the vast apartment.

And the curious thing about this mysterious cave was that, along one side of it, ran a long row of horse stalls, just like what one would find in a stable, and in each stall stood a coal-black charger, saddled and bridled, as if ready for the fray; and on the straw, by every horse's side, lay the gallant figure of a knight, clad from head to foot in coal-black armour, with a drawn sword in his mailed hand.

But not a horse moved, not a chain rattled. Knights and steeds alike were silent and motionless, looking exactly as if some strange enchantment had been thrown over them, and they had been suddenly turned into black marble.

There was something so awesome in the still, cold figures and in the unearthly silence that brooded over everything that Canonbie Dick, reckless and daring though he was, felt his courage waning and his knees beginning to shake under him.

In spite of these feelings, however, he followed the old man up the hall to the far end of it, where there was a table of ancient workmanship, on which was placed a glittering sword and a curiously wrought hunting-horn.

When they reached this table the stranger turned to him, and said, with great dignity, "Thou hast heard, good man, of Thomas of Ercildoune—Thomas the Rhymer, as men call him—he who went to dwell for a time with the Queen of Fairyland, and from her received the Gifts of Truth and Prophecy?"

Canonbie Dick nodded; for as the wonderful Soothsayer's name fell on his ears, his heart sank within him and his tongue seemed to cleave to the roof of his mouth. If he had been brought there to parley with Thomas the Rhymer, then had he laid himself open to all the eldrich Powers of Darkness.

"I that speak to thee am he," went on the white-haired stranger. "And I have permitted thee thus to have thy desire and follow me hither in order that I may try of what stuff thou art made. Before thee lies a Horn and a Sword. He that will sound the one, or draw the other, shall, if his courage fail not, be King over the whole of Britain. I, Thomas the Rhymer, have spoken it, and, as thou knowest, my tongue cannot lie. But list ye, the outcome of it all depends on thy bravery; and it will be a light task, or a heavy, according as thou layest hand on Sword or Horn first."

Now Dick was more versed in giving blows than in making music, and his first impulse was to seize the Sword, then, come what might, he had something in his hand to defend himself with. But just as he was about to lift it the thought struck him that, if the place were full of spirits, as he felt sure that it must be, this action of him might be taken to mean defiance, and might cause them to band themselves together against him.

So, changing his mind, he picked up the Horn with a trembling hand, and blew a blast upon it, which, however, was so weak and feeble that it could scarce be heard at the other end of the hall.

The result that followed was enough to appal the stoutest heart. Thunder rolled in crashing peals through the immense hall. The charmed Knights and their horses woke in an instant from their enchanted sleep. The Knights sprang to their feet and seized their swords, brandishing them round their heads, while their great black chargers stamped, and snorted, and ground their bits, as if eager to escape from their stalls. And where a moment before all had been stillness and silence, there was now a scene of wild din and excitement.

Now was the time for Canonbie Dick to play the man. If he had done so all the rest of his life might have been different.

But his courage failed him, and he lost his chance. Terrified at seeing so many threatening faces turned towards him, he dropped the Horn and made one weak, undecided effort to pick up the Sword.

But, ere he could do so, a mysterious voice sounded from

somewhere in the hall, and these were the words that it uttered:

"Woe to the coward, that ever he was born,

Who did not draw the Sword before he blew the Horn."

And, before Dick knew what he was about, a perfect whirlwind of cold, raw air tore through the cavern, carrying the luckless horse-dealer along with it; and, hurrying him along the narrow passage through which he had entered, dashed him down outside on a bank of loose stones and shale. He fell right to the bottom, and was found, with little life left in him, next morning, by some shepherds, to whom he had just strength enough left to whisper the story of his weird and fearful adventure.

THE MILK-WHITE DOO

There was once a man who got his living by working in the fields. He had one little son, called Curly-Locks, and one little daughter, called Golden-Tresses; but his wife was dead, and, as he had to be out all day, these children were often left alone. So, as he was afraid that some evil might befall them when there was no one to look after them, he, in an ill day, married again.

I say, "in an ill day," for his second wife was a most deceitful woman, who really hated children, although she pretended, before her marriage, to love them. And she was so unkind to them, and made the house so uncomfortable with her bad temper, that her poor husband often sighed to himself, and wished that he had let well alone, and remained a widower.

But it was no use crying over spilt milk; the deed was done, and he had just to try to make the best of it. So things went on for several years, until the children were beginning to run about the doors and play by themselves.

Then one day the Goodman chanced to catch a hare, and he brought it home and gave it to his wife to cook for the dinner.

Now his wife was a very good cook, and she made the hare into a pot of delicious soup; but she was also very greedy, and while the soup was boiling she tasted it, and tasted it, till at last she discovered that it was almost gone. Then she was in a fine state of mind, for she knew that her husband would soon be coming home for his dinner, and that she would have nothing to set before him.

So what do you think the wicked woman did? She went out to the door, where her little step-son, Curly-Locks, was playing in the sun, and told him to come in and get his face washed. And while she was washing his face, she struck him on the head with a hammer and stunned him, and popped him into the pot to make soup for his father's dinner.

By and by the Goodman came in from his work, and the soup was dished up; and he, and his wife, and his little daughter, Golden-Tresses, sat down to sup it.

"Where's Curly-Locks?" asked the Goodman. "It's a pity he is not here as long as the soup is hot."

"How should I ken?" answered his wife crossly. "I have other work to do than to run about after a mischievous laddie all the morning."

The Goodman went on supping his soup in silence for some minutes; then he lifted up a little foot in his spoon.

"This is Curly-Locks' foot," he cried in horror. "There hath been ill work here."

"Hoots, havers," answered his wife, laughing, pretending to be very much amused. "What should Curly-Locks' foot be doing in the soup? 'Tis the hare's forefoot, which is very like that of a bairn."

But presently the Goodman took something else up in his spoon.

"This is Curly-Locks' hand," he said shrilly. "I ken it by the crook in its little finger."

"The man's demented," retorted his wife, "not to ken the hind foot of a hare when he sees it!"

So the poor father did not say any more, but went away out to his work, sorely perplexed in his mind; while his little daughter, Golden-Tresses, who had a shrewd suspicion of what had happened, gathered all the bones from the empty plates, and, carrying them away in her apron, buried them beneath a flat stone, close by a white rose tree that grew by the cottage door.

And, lo and behold! those poor bones, which she buried with such care:

> *"Grew and grew,*
> *To a milk-white Doo,*
> *That took its wings,*
> *And away it flew."*

And at last it lighted on a tuft of grass by a burnside, where two women were washing clothes. It sat there cooing to itself for some time; then it sang this song softly to them:

> *"Pew, pew,*
> *My mimmie me slew,*
> *My daddy me chew,*
> *My sister gathered my banes,*
> *And put them between two milk-white stanes.*
> *And I grew and grew*
> *To a milk-white Doo,*
> *And I took to my wings and away I flew."*

The women stopped washing and looked at one another in astonishment. It was not every day that they came across a bird that could sing a song like that, and they felt that there was something not canny about it.

"Sing that song again, my bonnie bird," said one of them at last, "and we'll give thee all these clothes!"

So the bird sang its song over again, and the washerwomen gave it all the clothes, and it tucked them under its right wing, and flew on.

Presently it came to a house where all the windows were open, and it perched on one of the window-sills, and inside it saw a man counting out a great heap of silver.

And, sitting on the window-sill, it sang its song to him:

"Pew, pew,
My mimmie me slew,
My daddy me chew,
My sister gathered my banes,
And put them between two milk-white stanes.
And I grew and grew
To a milk-white Doo,
And I took to my wings and away I flew."

The man stopped counting his silver, and listened. He felt, like the washerwomen, that there was something not canny about this Doo. When it had finished its song, he said:

"Sing that song again, my bonnie bird, and I'll give thee a' this siller in a bag."

So the Doo sang its song over again, and got the bag of silver, which it tucked under its left wing. Then it flew on.

It had not flown very far, however, before it came to a mill where two millers were grinding corn. And it settled down on a sack of meal and sang its song to them.

"Pew, pew,
My mimmie me slew,
My daddy me chew,
My sister gathered my banes,
And put them between two milk-white stanes.
And I grew and grew
To a milk-white Doo,
And I took to my wings and away I flew."

The millers stopped their work, and looked at one another, scratching their heads in amazement.

"Sing that song over again, my bonnie bird!" exclaimed both of them together when the Doo had finished, "and we will give thee this millstone."

So the Doo repeated its song, and got the millstone, which it asked one of the millers to lift on its back; then it flew out of the mill, and up the valley, leaving the two men staring after it dumb with astonishment.

As you may think, the Milk-White Doo had a heavy load to carry, but it went bravely on till it came within sight of its father's cottage, and lighted down at last on the thatched roof.

Then it laid its burdens on the thatch, and, flying down to the courtyard, picked up a number of little chuckie stones. With them in its beak it flew back to the roof, and began to throw them down the chimney.

By this time it was evening, and the Goodman and his wife, and his little daughter, Golden-Tresses, were sitting round the table eating their supper. And you may be sure that they were all very much startled when the stones came rattling down the chimney, bringing such a cloud of soot with them that they were like to be smothered. They all jumped up from their chairs, and ran outside to see what the matter was.

And Golden-Tresses, being the littlest, ran the fastest, and when she came out at the door the Milk-White Doo flung the bundle of clothes down at her feet.

And the father came out next, and the Milk-White Doo flung the bag of silver down at his feet.

But the wicked step-mother, being somewhat stout came out last, and the Milk-White Doo threw the millstone right down on her head and killed her.

Then it spread its wings and flew away, and has never been seen again; but it had made the Goodman and his daughter rich for life, and it had rid them of the cruel step-mother, so that they lived in peace and plenty for the remainder of their days.

THE DRAIGLIN' HOGNEY

There was once a man who had three sons, and very little money to provide for them. So, when the eldest had grown into a lad, and saw that there was no means of making a livelihood at home, he went to his father and said to him:

"Father, if thou wilt give me a horse to ride on, a hound to hunt with, and a hawk to fly, I will go out into the wide world and seek my fortune."

His father gave him what he asked for; and he set out on his travels. He rode and he rode, over mountain and glen, until, just at nightfall, he came to a thick, dark wood. He entered it, thinking that he might find a path that would lead him through it; but no path was visible, and after wandering up and down for some time, he was obliged to acknowledge to himself that he was completely lost.

There seemed to be nothing for it but to tie his horse to a tree, and make a bed of leaves for himself on the ground; but just as he was about to do so he saw a light glimmering in the distance, and, riding on in the direction in which it was, he soon came to a clearing in the wood, in which stood a magnificent Castle.

The windows were all lit up, but the great door was barred; and, after he had ridden up to it, and knocked, and received no answer, the young man raised his hunting horn to his lips and blew a loud blast in the hope of letting the inmates know that he was without.

Instantly the door flew open of its own accord, and the young man entered, wondering very much what this strange thing would mean. And he wondered still more when he passed from room to room, and found that, although fires were burning brightly everywhere, and there was a plentiful meal laid out on the table in the great hall, there did not seem to be a single person in the whole of the vast building.

However, as he was cold, and tired, and wet, he put his horse in one of the stalls of the enormous stable, and taking his hawk and hound along with him, went into the hall and ate a hearty supper. After which he sat down by the side of the fire, and began to dry his clothes.

By this time it had grown late, and he was just thinking of retiring to one of the bedrooms which he had seen upstairs and going to bed, when a clock which was hanging on the wall struck twelve.

Instantly the door of the huge apartment opened, and a most awful-looking Draiglin' Hogney entered. His hair was matted and his beard was long, and his eyes shone like stars of fire from under his bushy eyebrows, and in his hands he carried a queerly shaped club.

He did not seem at all astonished to see his unbidden guest; but, coming across the hall, he sat down upon the opposite side of the fireplace, and, resting his chin on his hands, gazed fixedly at him.

"Doth thy horse ever kick any?" he said at last, in a harsh, rough voice.

"Ay, doth he," replied the young man; for the only steed that his father had been able to give him was a wild and unbroken colt.

"I have some skill in taming horses," went on the Draiglin' Hogney, "and I will give thee something to tame thine withal. Throw this over him"—and he pulled one of the long, coarse hairs out of his head and gave it to the young man. And there was something so commanding in the Hogney's voice that he did as he was bid, and went out to the stable and threw the hair over the horse.

Then he returned to the hall, and sat down again by the fire. The moment that he was seated the Draiglin' Hogney asked another question.

"Doth thy hound ever bite any?"

"Ay, verily," answered the youth; for his hound was so fierce-tempered that no man, save his master, dare lay a hand on him.

"I can cure the wildest tempered dog in Christendom," replied the Draiglin' Hogney. "Take that, and throw it over him." And he pulled another hair out of his head and gave it to the young man, who lost no time in flinging it over his hound.

There was still a third question to follow. "Doth ever thy hawk peck any?"

The young man laughed. "I have ever to keep a bandage over her eyes, save when she is ready to fly," said he; "else were nothing safe within her reach."

"Things will be safe now," said the Hogney, grimly. "Throw that over her." And for the third time he pulled a hair from his head and handed it to his companion. And as the other hairs had been thrown over the horse and the hound, so this one was thrown over the hawk.

Then, before the young man could draw breath, the fiercesome Draiglin' Hogney had given him such a clout on the side of his head with his queer-shaped club that he fell down in a heap on the floor.

And very soon his hawk and his hound tumbled down still and motionless beside him; and, out in the stable, his horse became stark and stiff, as if turned to stone. For the Draiglin's words had meant more than at first appeared when he said that he could make all unruly animals quiet.

Some time afterwards the second of the three sons came to his father in the old home with the same request that his brother had made. That he should be provided with a horse, a hawk, and a hound, and be allowed to go out to seek his fortune. And his father listened to him, and gave him what he asked, as he had given his brother.

And the young man set out, and in due time came to the wood, and lost himself in it, just as his brother had done; then he saw the light, and came to the Castle, and went in, and had supper, and dried his clothes, just as it all had happened before.

And the Draiglin' Hogney came in, and asked him the three questions, and he gave the same three answers, and received three hairs—one to throw over his horse, one to throw over his hound, and one to throw over his hawk; then the Hogney killed him, just as he had killed his brother.

Time passed, and the youngest son, finding that his two elder brothers never returned, asked his father for a horse, a hawk, and a hound, in order that he might go and look for them. And the poor old man, who was feeling very desolate in his old age, gladly gave them to him.

So he set out on his quest, and at nightfall he came, as the others had done, to the thick wood and the Castle. But, being a wise and cautious youth, he liked not the way in which he found things. He liked not the empty house; he liked not the spread-out feast; and, most of all, he liked not the look of the Draiglin' Hogney when he saw him. And he determined to be very careful what he said or did as long as he was in his company.

So when the Draiglin' Hogney asked him if his horse

kicked, he replied that it did, in very few words; and when he got one of the Hogney's hairs to throw over him, he went out to the stable, and pretended to do so, but he brought it back, hidden in his hand, and, when his unchancy companion was not looking, he threw it into the fire. It fizzled up like a tongue of flame with a little hissing sound like that of a serpent.

"What's that fizzling?" asked the Giant suspiciously.

"'Tis but the sap of the green wood," replied the young man carelessly, as he turned to caress his hound.

The answer satisfied the Draiglin' Hogney, and he paid no heed to the sound which the hair that should have been thrown over the hound, or the sound which the hair that should have been thrown over the hawk, made, when the young man threw them into the fire; and they fizzled up in the same way that the first had done.

Then, thinking that he had the stranger in his power, he whisked across the hearthstone to strike him with his club, as he had struck his brothers; but the young man was on the outlook, and when he saw him coming he gave a shrill whistle. And his horse, which loved him dearly, came galloping in from the stable, and his hound sprang up from the hearthstone where he had been sleeping; and his hawk, who was sitting on his shoulder, ruffled up her feathers and screamed harshly; and they all fell on the Draiglin' Hogney at once, and he found out only too well how the horse kicked, and the hound bit, and the hawk pecked; for they kicked him, and bit him, and pecked him, till he was as dead as a door nail.

When the young man saw that he was dead, he took his little club from his hand, and, armed with that, he set out to explore the Castle.

As he expected, he found that there were dark and dreary

dungeons under it, and in one of them he found his two brothers, lying cold and stiff side by side. He touched them with the club, and instantly they came to life again, and sprang to their feet as well as ever.

Then he went into another dungeon; and there were the two horses, and the two hawks, and the two hounds, lying as if dead, exactly as their Masters had lain. He touched them with his magic club, and they, too, came to life again.

Then he called to his two brothers, and the three young men searched the other dungeons, and they found great stores of gold and silver hidden in them, enough to make them rich for life.

So they buried the Draiglin' Hogney, and took possession of the Castle; and two of them went home and brought their old father back with them, and they all were as prosperous and happy as they could be; and, for aught that I know, they are living there still.

THE BROWNIE O'
FERNE-DEN

There have been many Brownies known in Scotland; and stories have been written about the Brownie o' Bodsbeck and the Brownie o' Blednock, but about neither of them has a prettier story been told than that which I am going to tell you about the Brownie o' Ferne-Den.

Now, Ferne-Den was a farmhouse, which got its name from the glen, or "den," on the edge of which it stood, and through which anyone who wished to reach the dwelling had to pass.

And this glen was believed to be the abode of a Brownie, who never appeared to anyone in the daytime, but who, it was said, was sometimes seen at night, stealing about, like an ungainly shadow, from tree to tree, trying to keep from observation, and never, by any chance, harming anybody.

Indeed, like all Brownies that are properly treated and let alone, so far was he from harming anybody that he was always on the look-out to do a good turn to those who needed his assistance. The farmer often said that he did not know what he would do without him; for if there was any work to be finished in a hurry at the farm—corn to thrash, or winnow, or tie up into bags, turnips to cut, clothes to wash, a kirn to be kirned, a garden to be weeded—all that the farmer and his wife had to do was to leave the door of the barn, or the turnip shed, or the milk house open when they went to bed, and put down a bowl of new milk on the doorstep for the Brownie's supper, and when they woke the next morning the bowl would be empty, and the job finished better than if it had been done by mortal hands.

In spite of all this, however, which might have proved to them how gentle and kindly the Creature really was, everyone about the place was afraid of him, and would rather go a couple of miles round about in the dark, when they were coming home from Kirk or Market, than pass through the glen, and run the risk of catching a glimpse of him.

I said that they were all afraid of him, but that was not true, for the farmer's wife was so good and gentle that she was not afraid of anything on God's earth, and when the Brownie's supper had to be left outside, she always filled his bowl with the richest milk, and added a good spoonful of cream to it, for, said she, "He works so hard for us, and asks no wages, he well deserves the very best meal that we can give him."

One night this gentle lady was taken very ill, and everyone was afraid that she was going to die. Of course, her husband was greatly distressed, and so were her servants, for she had been such a good Mistress to them that they loved her as if she had been their mother. But they were all young, and none of them knew very much about illness, and everyone agreed that it would be better to send off for an old woman who lived about seven miles away on the other side of the river, who was known to be a very skilful nurse.

But who was to go? That was the question. For it was black midnight, and the way to the old woman's house lay straight through the glen. And whoever travelled that road ran the risk of meeting the dreaded Brownie.

The farmer would have gone only too willingly, but he dare not leave his wife alone; and the servants stood in groups about the kitchen, each one telling the other that he ought to go, yet no one offering to go themselves.

Little did they think that the cause of all their terror, an odd, wee, misshapen little man, all covered with hair, with a long beard, red-rimmed eyes, broad, flat feet, just like the feet of a paddock, and enormous long arms that touched the ground, even when he stood upright, was within a yard or two of them, listening to their talk, with an anxious face, behind the kitchen door.

For he had come up as usual, from his hiding-place in the glen, to see if there were any work for him to do, and to look for his bowl of milk. And he had seen, from the open door and lit-up windows, that there was something wrong inside the farmhouse, which at that hour was wont to be dark, and still, and silent; and he had crept into the entry to try and find out what the matter was.

When he gathered from the servants' talk that the Mistress, whom he loved so dearly, and who had been so kind to him, was ill, his heart sank within him; and when he heard that the silly servants were so taken up with their own fears that they dared not set out to fetch a nurse for her, his contempt and anger knew no bounds.

"Fools, idiots, dolts!" he muttered to himself, stamping his odd, misshapen feet on the floor. "They speak as if a body were ready to take a bite off them as soon as ever he met them. If they only knew the bother it gives me to keep out of their road they wouldna be so silly. But, by my troth, if they go on like this, the bonnie lady will die amongst their fingers. So it strikes me that Brownie must e'en gang himself."

So saying, he reached up his hand, and took down a dark cloak which belonged to the farmer, which was hanging on a peg on the wall, and, throwing it over his head and shoulders, or as somewhat to hide his ungainly form, he hurried away to the stable, and saddled and bridled the fleetest-footed horse that stood there.

When the last buckle was fastened, he led it to the door and scrambled on its back. "Now, if ever thou travelledst fleetly, travel fleetly now," he said; and it was as if the creature understood him, for it gave a little whinny and pricked up its ears; then it darted out into the darkness like an arrow from the bow.

In less time than the distance had ever been ridden in before, the Brownie drew rein at the old woman's cottage.

She was in bed, fast asleep; but he rapped sharply on the window, and when she rose and put her old face, framed in its white mutch, close to the pane to ask who was there, he bent forward and told her his errand.

"Thou must come with me, Goodwife, and that quickly," he commanded, in his deep, harsh voice, "if the Lady of Ferne-Den's life is to be saved; for there is no one to nurse her up-bye at the farm there, save a lot of empty-headed servant wenches."

"But how am I to get there? Have they sent a cart for me?" asked the old woman anxiously; for, as far as she could see, there was nothing at the door save a horse and its rider.

"No, they have sent no cart," replied the Brownie, shortly. "So you must just climb up behind me on the saddle, and hang on tight to my waist, and I'll promise to land ye at Ferne-Den safe and sound."

His voice was so masterful that the old woman dare not refuse to do as she was bid; besides, she had often ridden pillion-wise when she was a lassie, so she made haste to dress herself, and when she was ready she unlocked her door, and, mounting the louping-on stane that stood beside it, she was soon seated behind the dark-cloaked stranger, with her arms clasped tightly round him.

Not a word was spoken till they approached the dreaded glen, then the old woman felt her courage giving way. "Do ye think that there will be any chance of meeting the Brownie?" she asked timidly. "I would fain not run the risk, for folk say that he is an unchancy creature."

Her companion gave a curious laugh. "Keep up your heart, and dinna talk havers," he said, "for I promise ye ye'll see naught uglier this night than the man whom ye ride behind."

"Oh, then, I'm fine and safe," replied the old woman, with a sigh of relief; "for although I havena' seen your face, I warrant that ye are a true man, for the care you have taken of a poor old woman."

She relapsed into silence again till the glen was passed and the good horse had turned into the farmyard. Then the horseman slid to the ground, and, turning round, lifted her carefully down in his long, strong arms. As he did so the cloak slipped off him, revealing his short, broad body and his misshapen limbs.

"In a' the world, what kind o' man are ye?" she asked, peering into his face in the grey morning light, which was just dawning. "What makes your eyes so big? And what have ye done to your feet? They are more like paddock's webs than aught else."

The odd little man laughed again. "I've wandered many

a mile in my time without a horse to help me, and I've heard it said that ower much walking makes the feet unshapely," he replied. "But waste no time in talking, good Dame. Go thy way into the house; and, hark'ee, if anyone asks thee who brought thee hither so quickly, tell them that there was a lack of men, so thou hadst e'en to be content to ride behind the BROWNIE O' FERNE-DEN."

THE WITCH OF FIFE

In the Kingdom of Fife, in the days of long ago, there lived an old man and his wife. The old man was a douce, quiet body, but the old woman was lightsome and flighty, and some of the neighbours were wont to look at her askance, and whisper to each other that they sorely feared that she was a Witch.

And her husband was afraid of it, too, for she had a curious habit of disappearing in the gloaming and staying out all night; and when she returned in the morning she looked quite white and tired, as if she had been travelling far, or working hard.

He used to try and watch her carefully, in order to find out where she went, or what she did, but he never managed to do so, for she always slipped out of the door when he was not looking, and before he could reach it to follow her, she had vanished utterly.

At last, one day, when he could stand the uncertainty no longer, he asked her to tell him straight out whether she were a Witch or no. And his blood ran cold when, without the slightest hesitation, she answered that she was; and if he would promise not to let anyone know, the next time that she went on one of her midnight expeditions she would tell him all about it.

The Goodman promised; for it seemed to him just as well that he should know all about his wife's cantrips.

He had not long to wait before he heard of them. For the very next week the moon was new, which is, as everybody knows, the time of all others when Witches like to stir abroad; and on the first night of the new moon his wife vanished. Nor did she return till daybreak next morning.

And when he asked her where she had been, she told him, in great glee, how she and four like-minded companions had met at the old Kirk on the moor and had mounted branches of the green bay tree and stalks of hemlock, which had instantly changed into horses, and how they had ridden, swift as the wind, over the country, hunting the foxes, and the weasels, and the owls; and how at last they had swam the Forth and come to the top of Bell Lomond. And how there they had dismounted from their horses, and drunk beer that had been brewed in no earthly brewery, out of horn cups that had been fashioned by no mortal hands.

And how, after that, a wee, wee man had jumped up from under a great mossy stone, with a tiny set of bagpipes under his arm, and how he had piped such wonderful music, that, at the sound of it, the very trouts jumped out of the Loch below, and the stoats crept out of their holes, and the corby crows and the herons came and sat on the trees in the darkness, to listen. And how all the Witches danced until they were so weary that, when the time came for them to mount their steeds again, if they would be home before cock-crow, they could scarce sit on them for fatigue.

The Goodman listened to this long story in silence, shaking his head meanwhile, and, when it was finished, all that he answered was: "And what the better are ye for all your dancing? Ye'd have been a deal more comfortable at home."

At the next new moon the old wife went off again for the night; and when she returned in the morning she told her husband how, on this occasion, she and her friends had taken cockle-shells for boats, and had sailed away over the stormy sea till they reached Norway. And there they had mounted invisible horses of wind, and had ridden and ridden, over mountains and glens, and glaciers, till they reached the land of the Lapps lying under its mantle of snow.

And here all the Elves, and Fairies, and Mermaids of the North were holding festival with Warlocks, and Brownies, and Pixies, and even the Phantom Hunters themselves, who are never looked upon by mortal eyes. And the Witches from Fife held festival with them, and danced, and feasted, and sang with them, and, what was of more consequence, they learned from them certain wonderful words, which, when they uttered them, would bear them through the air, and would undo all bolts and bars, and so gain them admittance to any place so-ever where they wanted to be. And after that they had come home again, delighted with the knowledge which they had acquired.

"What took ye to siccan a land as that?" asked the old man, with a contemptuous grunt. "Ye would hae been a sight warmer in your bed."

But when his wife returned from her next adventure, he showed a little more interest in her doings.

For she told him how she and her friends had met in the cottage of one of their number, and how, having heard that the Lord Bishop of Carlisle had some very rare wine in his cellar, they had placed their feet on the crook from which the pot hung, and had pronounced the magic words which they had learned from the Elves of Lappland. And, lo and behold! they flew up the chimney like whiffs of smoke, and sailed through the air like little wreathes of cloud, and in less time than it takes to tell they landed at the Bishop's Palace at Carlisle.

And the bolts and the bars flew loose before them, and they went down to his cellar and sampled his wine, and were back in Fife, fine, sober, old women by cock-crow.

When he heard this, the old man started from his chair in right earnest, for he loved good wine above all things, and it was but seldom that it came his way.

"By my troth, but thou art a wife to be proud of!" he cried. "Tell me the words, Woman! and I will e'en go and sample his Lordship's wine for myself."

But the Goodwife shook her head. "Na, na! I cannot do that," she said, "for if I did, an' ye telled it over again, 'twould turn the whole world upside down. For everybody would be leaving their own lawful work, and flying about the world after other folk's business and other folk's dainties. So just bide content, Goodman. Ye get on fine with the knowledge ye already possess."

And although the old man tried to persuade her with all the soft words he could think of, she would not tell him her secret.

But he was a sly old man, and the thought of the Bishop's wine gave him no rest. So night after night he went and hid in the old woman's cottage, in the hope that his wife and her friends would meet there; and although for a long time it was all in vain, at last his trouble was rewarded. For one evening the whole five old women assembled, and in low tones and with chuckles of laughter they recounted all that had befallen them in Lappland. Then, running to the fireplace, they, one after another, climbed on a chair and put their feet on the sooty crook. Then they repeated the magic words, and, hey, presto! they were up the lum and away before the old man could draw his breath.

"I can do that, too," he said to himself; and he crawled out of his hiding-place and ran to the fire. He put his foot on the crook and repeated the words, and up the chimney he went, and flew through the air after his wife and her companions, as if he had been a Warlock born.

And, as Witches are not in the habit of looking over their shoulders, they never noticed that he was following them, until they reached the Bishop's Palace and went down into his cellar, then, when they found that he was among them, they were not too well pleased.

However, there was no help for it, and they settled down to enjoy themselves. They tapped this cask of wine, and they tapped that, drinking a little of each, but not too much; for they were cautious old women, and they knew that if they wanted to get home before cock-crow it behoved them to keep their heads clear.

But the old man was not so wise, for he sipped, and he sipped, until at last he became quite drowsy, and lay down on the floor and fell fast asleep.

And his wife, seeing this, thought that she would teach him a lesson not to be so curious in the future. So, when she and her four friends thought that it was time to be gone, she departed without waking him.

He slept peacefully for some hours, until two of the Bishop's servants, coming down to the cellar to draw wine for their Master's table, almost fell over him in the darkness. Greatly astonished at his presence there, for the cellar door was fast locked, they dragged him up to the light and shook him, and cuffed him, and asked him how he came to be there.

And the poor old man was so confused at being awakened in this rough way, and his head seemed to whirl round so fast, that all he could stammer out was, "that he came from Fife, and that he had travelled on the midnight wind."

As soon as they heard that, the men servants cried out

that he was a Warlock, and they dragged him before the Bishop, and, as Bishops in those days had a holy horror of Warlocks and Witches, he ordered him to be burned alive.

When the sentence was pronounced, you may be very sure that the poor old man wished with all his heart that he had stayed quietly at home in bed, and never hankered after the Bishop's wine.

But it was too late to wish that now, for the servants dragged him out into the courtyard, and put a chain round his waist, and fastened it to a great iron stake, and they piled faggots of wood round his feet and set them alight.

As the first tiny little tongue of flame crept up, the poor old man thought that his last hour had come. But when he thought that, he forgot completely that his wife was a Witch.

For, just as the little tongue of flame began to singe his breeches, there was a swish and a flutter in the air, and a great Grey Bird, with outstretched wings, appeared in the sky, and swooped down suddenly, and perched for a moment on the old man's shoulder.

And in this Grey Bird's mouth was a little red pirnie, which, to everyone's amazement, it popped on to the prisoner's head. Then it gave one fierce croak, and flew away again, but to the old man's ears that croak was the sweetest music that he had ever heard.

For to him it was the croak of no earthly bird, but the voice of his wife whispering words of magic to him. And when he heard them he jumped for joy, for he knew that they were words of deliverance, and he shouted them aloud, and his chains fell off, and he mounted in the air—up and up—while the onlookers watched him in awestruck silence.

He flew right away to the Kingdom of Fife, without as

much as saying good-bye to them; and when he found himself once more safely at home, you may be very sure that he never tried to find out his wife's secrets again, but left her alone to her own devices.

ASSIPATTLE AND THE MESTER STOORWORM

In far bygone days, in the North, there lived a well-to-do farmer, who had seven sons and one daughter. And the youngest of these seven sons bore a very curious name; for men called him Assipattle, which means, "He who grovels among the ashes."

Perhaps Assipattle deserved his name, for he was rather a lazy boy, who never did any work on the farm as his brothers did, but ran about the doors with ragged clothes and unkempt hair, and whose mind was ever filled with wondrous stories of Trolls and Giants, Elves and Goblins.

When the sun was hot in the long summer afternoons, when the bees droned drowsily and even the tiny insects seemed almost asleep, the boy was content to throw himself down on the ash-heap amongst the ashes, and lie there, lazily letting them run through his fingers, as one might play with sand on the sea-shore, basking in the sunshine and telling stories to himself.

And his brothers, working hard in the fields, would point to him with mocking fingers, and laugh, and say to each other how well the name suited him, and of how little use he was in the world.

And when they came home from their work, they would push him about and tease him, and even his mother would make him sweep the floor, and draw water from the well, and fetch peats from the peat-stack, and do all the little odd jobs that nobody else would do.

So poor Assipattle had rather a hard life of it, and he would often have been very miserable had it not been for his sister, who loved him dearly, and who would listen quite patiently to all the stories that he had to tell; who never laughed at him or told him that he was telling lies, as his brothers did.

But one day a very sad thing happened—at least, it was a sad thing for poor Assipattle.

For it chanced that the King of these parts had one only daughter, the Princess Gemdelovely, whom he loved dearly, and to whom he denied nothing. And Princess Gemdelovely was in want of a waiting-maid, and as she had seen Assipattle's sister standing by the garden gate as she was riding by one day, and had taken a fancy to her, she asked her father if she might ask her to come and live at the Castle and serve her.

Her father agreed at once, as he always did agree to any of her wishes; and sent a messenger in haste to the farmer's house to ask if his daughter would come to the Castle to be the Princess's waiting-maid.

And, of course, the farmer was very pleased at the piece of good fortune which had befallen the girl, and so was her mother, and so were her six brothers, all except poor Assipattle, who looked with wistful eyes after his sister as she rode away, proud of her new clothes and of the rivlins which her father had made her out of cowhide, which she was to wear in the Palace when she waited on the Princess, for at home she always ran barefoot.

Time passed, and one day a rider rode in hot haste through the country bearing the most terrible tidings. For the evening before, some fishermen, out in their boats, had caught sight of the Mester Stoorworm, which, as everyone knows, was the largest, and the first, and the greatest of all Sea-Serpents. It was that beast which, in the Good Book, is called the Leviathan, and if it had been measured in our day, its tail would have touched Iceland, while its snout rested on the North Cape.

And the fishermen had noticed that this fearsome Monster had its head turned towards the mainland, and that it opened its mouth and yawned horribly, as if to show that it was hungry, and that, if it were not fed, it would kill every living thing upon the land, both man and beast, bird and creeping thing.

For 'twas well known that its breath was so poisonous that it consumed as with a burning fire everything that it lighted on. So that, if it pleased the awful creature to lift its head and put forth its breath, like noxious vapour, over the country, in a few weeks the fair land would be turned into a region of desolation.

As you may imagine, everyone was almost paralysed with terror at this awful calamity which threatened them; and the King called a solemn meeting of all his Counsellors, and asked them if they could devise any way of warding off the danger.

And for three whole days they sat in Council, these grave, bearded men, and many were the suggestions which were made, and many the words of wisdom which were spoken; but, alas! no one was wise enough to think of a way by which the Mester Stoorworm might be driven back.

At last, at the end of the third day, when everyone had given up hope of finding a remedy, the door of the Council Chamber opened and the Queen appeared.

Now the Queen was the King's second wife, and she was not a favourite in the Kingdom, for she was a proud, insolent woman, who did not behave kindly to her step-daughter, the

Princess Gemdelovely, and who spent much more of her time in the company of a great Sorcerer, whom everyone feared and dreaded, than she did in that of the King, her husband.

So the sober Counsellors looked at her disapprovingly as she came boldly into the Council Chamber and stood up beside the King's Chair of State, and, speaking in a loud, clear voice, addressed them thus:

"Ye think that ye are brave men and strong, oh, ye Elders, and fit to be the Protectors of the People. And so it may be, when it is mortals that ye are called on to face. But ye be no match for the foe that now threatens our land. Before him your weapons be but as straw. 'Tis not through strength of arm, but through sorcery, that he will be overcome. So listen to my words, even though they be but those of a woman, and take counsel with the great Sorcerer, from whom nothing is hid, but who knoweth all the mysteries of the earth, and of the air, and of the sea."

Now the King and his Counsellors liked not this advice, for they hated the Sorcerer, who had, as they thought, too much influence with the Queen; but they were at their wits' end, and knew not to whom to turn for help, so they were fain to do as she said and summon the Wizard before them.

And when he obeyed the summons and appeared in their midst, they liked him none the better for his looks. For he was long, and thin, and awesome, with a beard that came down to his knee, and hair that wrapped him about like a mantle, and his face was the colour of mortar, as if he had always lived in darkness, and had been afraid to look on the sun.

But there was no help to be found in any other man, so they laid the case before him, and asked him what they should do. And he answered coldly that he would think over the matter, and come again to the Assembly the following day and give them his advice.

And his advice, when they heard it, was like to turn their hair white with horror.

For he said that the only way to satisfy the Monster, and to make it spare the land, was to feed it every Saturday with seven young maidens, who must be the fairest who could be found; and if, after this remedy had been tried once or twice, it did not succeed in mollifying the Stoorworm and inducing him to depart, there was but one other measure that he could suggest, but that was so horrible and dreadful that he would not rend their hearts by mentioning it in the meantime.

And as, although they hated him, they feared him also, the Council had e'en to abide by his words, and pronounced the awful doom.

And so it came about that, every Saturday, seven bonnie, innocent maidens were bound hand and foot and laid on a rock which ran into the sea, and the Monster stretched out his long, jagged tongue, and swept them into his mouth; while all the rest of the folk looked on from the top of a high hill—or, at least, the men looked—with cold, set faces, while the women hid theirs in their aprons and wept aloud.

"Is there no other way," they cried, "no other way than this, to save the land?"

But the men only groaned and shook their heads. "No other way," they answered; "no other way."

Then suddenly a boy's indignant voice rang out among the crowd. "Is there no grown man who would fight that Monster, and kill him, and save the lassies alive? I would do it; I am not feared for the Mester Stoorworm."

It was the boy Assipattle who spoke, and everyone looked at him in amazement as he stood staring at the great Sea-Serpent, his fingers twitching with rage, and his great blue eyes glowing with pity and indignation.

"The poor bairn's mad; the sight hath turned his head," they whispered one to another; and they would have crowded round him to pet and comfort him, but his elder brother came and gave him a heavy clout on the side of his head.

"Thou fight the Stoorworm!" he cried contemptuously. "A likely story! Go home to thy ash-pit, and stop speaking havers;" and, taking his arm, he drew him to the place where his other brothers were waiting, and they all went home together.

But all the time Assipattle kept on saying that he meant to kill the Stoorworm; and at last his brothers became so angry at what they thought was mere bragging, that they picked up stones and pelted him so hard with them that at last he took to his heels and ran away from them.

That evening the six brothers were threshing corn in the barn, and Assipattle, as usual, was lying among the ashes thinking his own thoughts, when his mother came out and bade him run and tell the others to come in for their supper.

The boy did as he was bid, for he was a willing enough little fellow; but when he entered the barn his brothers, in revenge for his having run away from them in the afternoon, set on him and pulled him down, and piled so much straw on top of him that, had his father not come from the house to see what they were all waiting for, he would, of a surety, have been smothered.

But when, at supper-time, his mother was quarrelling

with the other lads for what they had done, and saying to them that it was only cowards who set on bairns littler and younger than themselves, Assipattle looked up from the bicker of porridge which he was supping.

"Vex not thyself, Mother," he said, "for I could have fought them all if I liked; ay, and beaten them, too."

"Why didst thou not essay it then?" cried everybody at once.

"Because I knew that I would need all my strength when I go to fight the Giant Stoorworm," replied Assipattle gravely.

And, as you may fancy, the others laughed louder than before.

Time passed, and every Saturday seven lassies were thrown to the Stoorworm, until at last it was felt that this state of things could not be allowed to go on any longer; for if it did, there would soon be no maidens at all left in the country.

So the Elders met once more, and, after long consultation, it was agreed that the Sorcerer should be summoned, and asked what his other remedy was. "For, by our troth," said they, "it cannot be worse than that which we are practising now."

But, had they known it, the new remedy was even more dreadful than the old. For the cruel Queen hated her step-daughter, Gemdelovely, and the wicked Sorcerer knew that she did, and that she would not be sorry to get rid of her, and, things being as they were, he thought that he saw a way to please the Queen. So he stood up in the Council, and, pretending to be very sorry, said that the only other thing that could be done was to give the Princess Gemdelovely to the Stoorworm, then would it of a surety depart.

When they heard this sentence a terrible stillness fell upon the Council, and everyone covered his face with his hands, for no man dare look at the King.

But although his dear daughter was as the apple of his eye, he was a just and righteous Monarch, and he felt that it was not right that other fathers should have been forced to part with their daughters, in order to try and save the country, if his child was to be spared.

So, after he had had speech with the Princess, he stood up before the Elders, and declared, with trembling voice, that both he and she were ready to make the sacrifice.

"She is my only child," he said, "and the last of her race. Yet it seemeth good to both of us that she should lay down her life, if by so doing she may save the land that she loves so well."

Salt tears ran down the faces of the great bearded men as they heard their King's words, for they all knew how dear the Princess Gemdelovely was to him. But it was felt that what he said was wise and true, and that the thing was just and right; for 'twere better, surely, that one maiden should die, even although she were of Royal blood, than that bands of other maidens should go to their death week by week, and all to no purpose.

So, amid heavy sobs, the aged Lawman—he who was the chief man of the Council—rose up to pronounce the Princess's doom. But, ere he did so, the King's Kemper—or Fighting-man—stepped forward.

"Nature teaches us that it is fitting that each beast hath a tail," he said; "and this Doom, which our Lawman is about to pronounce, is in very sooth a venomous beast. And, if I had my way, the tail which it would bear after it is this, that if the Mester Stoorworm doth not depart, and that right speedily, after he have devoured the Princess, the next thing that is offered to him be no tender young maiden, but that tough, lean old Sorcerer."

And at his words there was such a great shout of approval that the wicked Sorcerer seemed to shrink within himself, and his pale face grew paler than it was before.

Now, three weeks were allowed between the time that the Doom was pronounced upon the Princess and the time that it was carried out, so that the King might send Ambassadors to all the neighbouring Kingdoms to issue proclamations that, if any Champion would come forward who was able to drive away the Stoorworm and save the Princess, he should have her for his wife.

And with her he should have the Kingdom, as well as a very famous sword that was now in the King's possession, but which had belonged to the great god Odin, with which he had fought and vanquished all his foes.

The sword bore the name of Sickersnapper, and no man had any power against it.

The news of all these things spread over the length and breadth of the land, and everyone mourned for the fate that was like to befall the Princess Gemdelovely. And the farmer, and his wife, and their six sons mourned also;--all but Assipattle, who sat amongst the ashes and said nothing.

When the King's Proclamation was made known throughout the neighbouring Kingdoms, there was a fine stir among all the young Gallants, for it seemed but a little thing to slay a Sea-Monster; and a beautiful wife, a fertile Kingdom, and a trusty sword are not to be won every day.

So six-and-thirty Champions arrived at the King's Palace, each hoping to gain the prize.

But the King sent them all out to look at the Giant Stoorworm lying in the sea with its enormous mouth open, and when they saw it, twelve of them were seized with sudden illness, and twelve of them were so afraid that they took to their heels and ran, and never stopped till they reached their own countries; and so only twelve returned to the King's Palace, and as for them, they were so downcast at the thought of the task that they had undertaken that they had no spirit left in them at all.

And none of them dare try to kill the Stoorworm; so the three weeks passed slowly by, until the night before the day on which the Princess was to be sacrificed. On that night the King, feeling that he must do something to entertain his guests, made a great supper for them.

But, as you may think, it was a dreary feast, for everyone was thinking so much about the terrible thing that was to happen on the morrow, that no one could eat or drink.

And when it was all over, and everybody had retired to rest, save the King and his old Kemperman, the King returned to the great hall, and went slowly up to his Chair of State, high up on the dais. It was not like the Chairs of State that we know nowadays; it was nothing but a massive Kist, in which he kept all the things which he treasured most.

The old Monarch undid the iron bolts with trembling fingers, and lifted the lid, and took out the wondrous sword Sickersnapper, which had belonged to the great god Odin.

His trusty Kemperman, who had stood by him in a hundred fights, watched him with pitying eyes.

"Why lift ye out the sword," he said softly, "when thy fighting days are done? Right nobly hast thou fought thy battles in the past, oh, my Lord! when thine arm was strong and sure. But when folk's years number four score and sixteen, as thine do, 'tis time to leave such work to other and younger men."

The old King turned on him angrily, with something of the old fire in his eyes. "Wheest," he cried, "else will I turn this sword on thee. Dost thou think that I can see my only bairn devoured by a Monster, and not lift a finger to try and save her when no other man will? I tell thee—and I will swear it with my two thumbs crossed on Sickersnapper—that both the sword and I will be destroyed before so much as one of her hairs be touched. So go, an' thou love me, my old comrade, and order my boat to be ready, with the sail set and the prow pointed out to sea. I will go myself and fight the Stoorworm; and if I do not return, I will lay it on thee to guard my cherished daughter. Peradventure, my life may redeem hers."

Now that night everybody at the farm went to bed betimes, for next morning the whole family was to set out early, to go to the top of the hill near the sea, to see the Princess eaten by the Stoorworm. All except Assipattle, who was to be left at home to herd the geese.

The lad was so vexed at this—for he had great schemes in his head—that he could not sleep. And as he lay tossing and tumbling about in his corner among the ashes, he heard his father and mother talking in the great box-bed. And, as he listened, he found that they were having an argument.

"'Tis such a long way to the hill overlooking the sea, I fear me I shall never walk it," said his mother. "I think I had better bide at home."

"Nay," replied her husband, "that would be a bonny-like thing, when all the country-side is to be there. Thou shalt ride behind me on my good mare Go-Swift."

"I do not care to trouble thee to take me behind thee," said his wife, "for methinks thou dost not love me as thou wert wont to do."

"The woman's havering," cried the Goodman of the house impatiently. "What makes thee think that I have ceased to love thee?"

"Because thou wilt no longer tell me thy secrets," answered his wife. "To go no further, think of this very horse, Go-Swift. For five long years I have been begging thee to tell me how it is that, when thou ridest her, she flies faster than the wind, while if any other man mount her, she hirples along like a broken-down nag."

The Goodman laughed. "'Twas not for lack of love, Goodwife," he said, "though it might be lack of trust. For women's tongues wag but loosely; and I did not want other folk to ken my secret. But since my silence hath vexed thy heart, I will e'en tell it thee.

"When I want Go-Swift to stand, I give her one clap on the left shoulder. When I would have her go like any other horse, I give her two claps on the right. But when I want her to fly like the wind, I whistle through the windpipe of a goose. And, as I never ken when I want her to gallop like that, I aye keep the bird's thrapple in the left-hand pocket of my coat."

"So that is how thou managest the beast," said the farmer's wife, in a satisfied tone; "and that is what becomes of all my goose thrapples. Oh! but thou art a clever fellow, Goodman; and now that I ken the way of it I may go to sleep."

Assipattle was not tumbling about in the ashes now; he was sitting up in the darkness, with glowing cheeks and sparkling eyes.

His opportunity had come at last, and he knew it.

He waited patiently till their heavy breathing told him that his parents were asleep; then he crept over to where his father's clothes were, and took the goose's windpipe out of the pocket of his coat, and slipped noiselessly out of the house. Once he was out of it, he ran like lightning to the stable. He saddled and bridled Go-Swift, and threw a halter round her neck, and led her to the stable door.

The good mare, unaccustomed to her new groom, pranced, and reared, and plunged; but Assipattle, knowing his father's secret, clapped her once on the left shoulder, and she stood as still as a stone. Then he mounted her, and gave her two claps on the right shoulder, and the good horse trotted off briskly, giving a loud neigh as she did so.

The unwonted sound, ringing out in the stillness of the night, roused the household, and the Goodman and his six sons came tumbling down the wooden stairs, shouting to one another in confusion that someone was stealing Go-Swift.

The farmer was the first to reach the door; and when he saw, in the starlight, the vanishing form of his favourite steed, he cried at the top of his voice:

"Stop thief, ho!
Go-Swift, whoa!"

And when Go-Swift heard that she pulled up in a moment. All seemed lost, for the farmer and his sons could run very fast indeed, and it seemed to Assipattle, sitting motionless on Go-Swift's back, that they would very soon make up on him.

But, luckily, he remembered the goose's thrapple, and he pulled it out of his pocket and whistled through it. In an instant the good mare bounded forward, swift as the wind, and was over the hill and out of reach of its pursuers before they had taken ten steps more.

Day was dawning when the lad came within sight of the sea; and there, in front of him, in the water, lay the enormous Monster whom he had come so far to slay. Anyone would have said that he was mad even to dream of making such an attempt, for he was but a slim, unarmed youth, and the Mester Stoorworm was so big that men said it would reach the fourth part round the world. And its tongue was jagged at the end like a fork, and with this fork it could sweep whatever it chose into its mouth, and devour it at its leisure.

For all this, Assipattle was not afraid, for he had the heart of a hero underneath his tattered garments. "I must be cautious," he said to himself, "and do by my wits what I cannot do by my strength."

He climbed down from his seat on Go-Swift's back, and tethered the good steed to a tree, and walked on, looking well about him, till he came to a little cottage on the edge of a wood.

The door was not locked, so he entered, and found its occupant, an old woman, fast asleep in bed. He did not disturb her, but he took down an iron pot from the shelf, and examined it closely.

"This will serve my purpose," he said; "and surely the old dame would not grudge it if she knew 'twas to save the Princess's life."

Then he lifted a live peat from the smouldering fire, and went his way.

Down at the water's edge he found the King's boat lying, guarded by a single boatman, with its sails set and its prow turned in the direction of the Mester Stoorworm.

"It's a cold morning," said Assipattle. "Art thou not well-nigh frozen sitting there? If thou wilt come on shore, and run about, and warm thyself, I will get into the boat and guard it till thou returnest."

"A likely story," replied the man. "And what would the King say if he were to come, as I expect every moment he will do, and find me playing myself on the sand, and his good boat left to a smatchet like thee? 'Twould be as much as my head is worth."

"As thou wilt," answered Assipattle carelessly, beginning to search among the rocks. "In the meantime, I must be looking for a wheen mussels to roast for my breakfast." And after he had gathered the mussels, he began to make a hole in the sand to put the live peat in. The boatman watched him curiously, for he, too, was beginning to feel hungry.

Presently the lad gave a wild shriek, and jumped high in the air. "Gold, gold!" he cried. "By the name of Thor, who would have looked to find gold here?"

This was too much for the boatman. Forgetting all about his head and the King, he jumped out of the boat, and, pushing Assipattle aside, began to scrape among the sand with all his might.

While he was doing so, Assipattle seized his pot, jumped into the boat, pushed her off, and was half a mile out to sea before the outwitted man, who, needless to say, could find no gold, noticed what he was about.

And, of course, he was very angry, and the old King was more angry still when he came down to the shore, attended by his Nobles and carrying the great sword Sickersnapper, in the vain hope that he, poor feeble old man that he was, might be able in some way to defeat the Monster and save his daughter.

But to make such an attempt was beyond his power now that his boat was gone. So he could only stand on the shore, along with the fast assembling crowd of his subjects, and watch what would befall.

And this was what befell!

Assipattle, sailing slowly over the sea, and watching the Mester Stoorworm intently, noticed that the terrible Monster yawned occasionally, as if longing for his weekly feast. And as it yawned a great flood of sea-water went down its throat, and came out again at its huge gills.

So the brave lad took down his sail, and pointed the prow of his boat straight at the Monster's mouth, and the next time it yawned he and his boat were sucked right in, and, like Jonah, went straight down its throat into the dark regions inside its body. On and on the boat floated; but as it went the water grew less, pouring out of the Stoorworm's gills, till at last it stuck, as it were, on dry land. And Assipattle jumped out, his pot in his hand, and began to explore.

Presently he came to the huge creature's liver, and having heard that the liver of a fish is full of oil, he made a hole in it and put in the live peat.

Woe's me! but there was a conflagration! And Assipattle just got back to his boat in time; for the Mester Stoorworm, in its convulsions, threw the boat right out of its mouth again, and it was flung up, high and dry, on the bare land.

The commotion in the sea was so terrible that the King and his daughter—who by this time had come down to the shore dressed like a bride, in white, ready to be thrown to the Monster—and all his Courtiers, and all the country-folk, were fain to take refuge on the hill top, out of harm's way, and stand and see what happened next.

And this was what happened next.

The poor, distressed creature—for it was now to be pitied, even although it was a great, cruel, awful Mester Stoorworm—tossed itself to and fro, twisting and writhing.

And as it tossed its awful head out of the water its tongue fell out, and struck the earth with such force that it made a great dent in it, into which the sea rushed. And that dent formed the crooked Straits which now divide Denmark from Norway and Sweden.

Then some of its teeth fell out and rested in the sea, and became the Islands that we now call the Orkney Isles; and a little afterwards some more teeth dropped out, and they became what we now call the Shetland Isles.

After that the creature twisted itself into a great lump and died; and this lump became the Island of Iceland; and the fire which Assipattle had kindled with his live peat still burns on underneath it, and that is why there are mountains which throw out fire in that chilly land.

When at last it was plainly seen that the Mester Stoorworm was dead, the King could scarce contain himself with joy. He put his arms round Assipattle's neck, and kissed him, and called him his son. And he took off his own Royal Mantle and put it on the lad, and girded his good sword Sickersnapper round his waist. And he called his daughter, the Princess Gemdelovely, to him, and put her hand in his, and declared that when the right time came she should be his wife, and that he should be ruler over all the Kingdom.

Then the whole company mounted their horses again, and Assipattle rode on Go-Swift by the Princess's side; and so they returned, with great joy, to the King's Palace.

But as they were nearing the gate Assipattle's sister, she who was the Princess's maid, ran out to meet him, and signed to the Princess to lout down, and whispered something in her ear.

The Princess's face grew dark, and she turned her horse's head and rode back to where her father was, with his Nobles. She told him the words that the maiden had spoken; and when he heard them his face, too, grew as black as thunder.

For the matter was this: The cruel Queen, full of joy at the thought that she was to be rid, once for all, of her step-daughter, had been making love to the wicked Sorcerer all the morning in the old King's absence.

"He shall be killed at once," cried the Monarch. "Such behaviour cannot be overlooked."

"Thou wilt have much ado to find him, your Majesty," said the girl, "for 'tis more than an hour since he and the Queen fled together on the fleetest horses that they could find in the stables."

"But I can find him," cried Assipattle; and he went off like the wind on his good horse Go-Swift.

It was not long before he came within sight of the fugitives, and he drew his sword and shouted to them to stop.

They heard the shout, and turned round, and they both laughed aloud in derision when they saw that it was only the boy who grovelled in the ashes who pursued them.

"The insolent brat! I will cut off his head for him! I will teach him a lesson!" cried the Sorcerer; and he rode boldly back to meet Assipattle. For although he was no fighter, he knew that no ordinary weapon could harm his enchanted body; therefore he was not afraid.

But he did not count on Assipattle having the Sword of the great god Odin, with which he had slain all his enemies; and before this magic weapon he was powerless. And, at one thrust, the young lad ran it through his body as easily as if he had been any ordinary man, and he fell from his horse, dead.

Then the Courtiers of the King, who had also set off in pursuit, but whose steeds were less fleet of foot than Go-Swift, came up, and seized the bridle of the Queen's horse, and led it and its rider back to the Palace.

She was brought before the Council, and judged, and condemned to be shut up in a high tower for the remainder of her life. Which thing surely came to pass.

As for Assipattle, when the proper time came he was married to the Princess Gemdelovely, with great feasting and rejoicing. And when the old King died they ruled the Kingdom for many a long year.

THE FOX AND THE WOLF

There was once a Fox and a Wolf, who set up house together in a cave near the sea-shore. Although you may not think so, they got on very well for a time, for they went out hunting all day, and when they came back at night they were generally too tired to do anything but to eat their supper and go to bed.

They might have lived together always had it not been for the slyness and greediness of the Fox, who tried to over-reach his companion, who was not nearly so clever as he was.

And this was how it came about.

It chanced, one dark December night, that there was a dreadful storm at sea, and in the morning the beach was all strewn with wreckage. So as soon as it was daylight the two friends went down to the shore to see if they could find any-thing to eat.

They had the good fortune to light on a great Keg of But-ter, which had been washed overboard from some ship on its way home from Ireland, where, as all the world knows, folk are famous for their butter.

The simple Wolf danced with joy when he saw it. "Mar-rowbones and trotters! but we will have a good supper this night," cried he, licking his lips. "Let us set to work at once and roll it up to the cave."

But the wily Fox was fond of butter, and he made up his mind that he would have it all to himself. So he put on his wisest look, and shook his head gravely.

"Thou hast no prudence, my friend," he said reproach-fully, "else wouldst thou not talk of breaking up a Keg of But-ter at this time of year, when the stackyards are full of good grain, which can be had for the eating, and the farmyards are stocked with nice fat ducks and poultry. No, no. It behoveth us to have foresight, and to lay up in store for the spring, when the grain is all threshed, and the stackyards are bare, and the poultry have gone to market. So we will e'en bury the Keg, and dig it up when we have need of it."

Very reluctantly, for he was thinner and hungrier than the Fox, the Wolf agreed to this proposal. So a hole was dug, and the Keg was buried, and the two animals went off hunting as usual.

About a week passed by: then one day the Fox came into the cave, and flung himself down on the ground as if he were very much exhausted. But if anyone had looked at him closely they would have seen a sly twinkle in his eye.

"Oh, dear, oh, dear!" he sighed. "Life is a heavy burden."

"What hath befallen thee?" asked the Wolf, who was ever kind and soft-hearted.

"Some friends of mine, who live over the hills yonder, are wanting me to go to a christening to-night. Just think of the distance that I must travel."

"But needst thou go?" asked the Wolf. "Canst thou not send an excuse?"

"I doubt that no excuse would be accepted," answered the Fox, "for they asked me to stand god-father. Therefore it behoveth me to do my duty, and pay no heed to my own feelings."

So that evening the Fox was absent, and the Wolf was alone in the cave. But it was not to a christening that the sly Fox went; it was to the Keg of Butter that was buried in the sand. About midnight he returned, looking fat and sleek, and well pleased with himself.

The Wolf had been dozing, but he looked up drowsily as

his companion entered. "Well, how did they name the bairn?" he asked.

"They gave it a queer name," answered the Fox. "One of the queerest names that I ever heard."

"And what was that?" questioned the Wolf.

"Nothing less than 'Blaisean' (Let-me-taste)," replied the Fox, throwing himself down in his corner. And if the Wolf could have seen him in the darkness he would have noticed that he was laughing to himself.

Some days afterwards the same thing happened. The Fox was asked to another christening; this time at a place some twenty-five miles along the shore. And as he had grumbled before, so he grumbled again; but he declared that it was his duty to go, and he went.

At midnight he came back, smiling to himself and with no appetite for his supper. And when the Wolf asked him the name of the child, he answered that it was a more extraordinary name than the other—"Be na Inheadnon" (Be in its middle).

The very next week, much to the Wolf's wonder, the Fox was asked to yet another christening. And this time the name of the child was "Sgriot an Clar" (Scrape the staves). After that the invitations ceased.

Time went on, and the hungry spring came, and the Fox and the Wolf had their larder bare, for food was scarce, and the weather was bleak and cold.

"Let us go and dig up the Keg of Butter," said the Wolf. "Methinks that now is the time we need it."

The Fox agreed—having made up his mind how he would act—and the two set out to the place where the Keg had been hidden. They scraped away the sand, and uncovered it; but, needless to say, they found it empty.

"This is thy work," said the Fox angrily, turning to the poor, innocent Wolf. "Thou hast crept along here while I was at the christenings, and eaten it up by stealth."

"Not I," replied the Wolf. "I have never been near the spot since the day that we buried it together."

"But I tell thee it must have been thou," insisted the Fox, "for no other creature knew it was there except ourselves. And, besides, I can see by the sleekness of thy fur that thou hast fared well of late."

Which last sentence was both unjust and untrue, for the poor Wolf looked as lean and badly nourished as he could possibly be.

So back they both went to the cave, arguing all the way. The Fox declaring that the Wolf *must* have been the thief, and the Wolf protesting his innocence.

"Art thou ready to swear to it?" said the Fox at last; though why he asked such a question, dear only knows.

"Yes, I am," replied the Wolf firmly; and, standing in the middle of the cave, and holding one paw up solemnly he swore this awful oath:

"If it be that I stole the butter; if it be, if it be—
May a fateful, fell disease fall on me, fall on me."

When he was finished, he put down his paw and, turning to the Fox, looked at him keenly; for all at once it struck him that his fur looked sleek and fine.

"It is thy turn now," he said. "I have sworn, and thou must do so also."

The Fox's face fell at these words, for although he was

both untruthful and dishonest now, he had been well brought up in his youth, and he knew that it was a terrible thing to perjure oneself and swear falsely.

So he made one excuse after another, but the Wolf, who was getting more and more suspicious every moment, would not listen to him.

So, as he had not courage to tell the truth, he was forced at last to swear an oath also, and this was what he swore:

> *"If it be that I stole the butter; if it be, if it be—*
> *Then let some most deadly punishment fall on me,*
> *fall on me—*
> *Whirrum wheeckam, whirrum wheeckam,*
> *Whirram whee, whirram whee!"*

After he had heard him swear this terrible oath, the Wolf thought that his suspicions must be groundless, and he would have let the matter rest; but the Fox, having an uneasy conscience, could not do so. So he suggested that as it was clear that one of them must have eaten the Keg of Butter, they should both stand near the fire; so that when they became hot, the butter would ooze out of the skin of whichever of them was guilty. And he took care that the Wolf should stand in the hottest place.

But the fire was big and the cave was small; and while the poor lean Wolf showed no sign of discomfort, he himself, being nice and fat and comfortable, soon began to get unpleasantly warm.

As this did not suit him at all, he next proposed that they should go for a walk, "for," said he, "it is now quite plain that neither of us can have taken the butter. It must have been some stranger who hath found out our secret."

But the Wolf had seen the Fox beginning to grow greasy, and he knew now what had happened, and he determined to have his revenge. So he waited until they came to a smithy which stood at the side of the road, where a horse was waiting just outside the door to be shod.

Then, keeping at a safe distance, he said to his companion, "There is writing on that smithy door, which I cannot read, as my eyes are failing; do thou try to read it, for perchance it may be something 'twere good for us to know."

And the silly Fox, who was very vain, and did not like to confess that his eyes were no better than those of his friend, went close up to the door to try and read the writing. And he chanced to touch the horse's fetlock, and, it being a restive beast, lifted its foot and struck out at once, and killed the Fox as dead as a door-nail.

And so, you see, the old saying in the Good Book came true after all: "Be sure your sin will find you out."

KATHERINE CRACKERNUTS

There was once a King whose wife died, leaving him with an only daughter, whom he dearly loved. The little Princess's name was Velvet-Cheek, and she was so good, and bonnie, and kind-hearted that all her father's subjects loved her. But as the King was generally engaged in transacting the business of the State, the poor little maiden had rather a lonely life, and often wished that she had a sister with whom she could play, and who would be a companion to her.

The King, hearing this, made up his mind to marry a middle-aged Countess, whom he had met at a neighbouring Court, who had one daughter, named Katherine, who was just a little younger than the Princess Velvet-Cheek, and who, he thought, would make a nice play-fellow for her.

He did so, and in one way the arrangement turned out very well, for the two girls loved one another dearly, and had everything in common, just as if they had really been sisters.

But in another way it turned out very badly, for the new Queen was a cruel and ambitious woman, and she wanted her own daughter to do as she had done, and make a grand marriage, and perhaps even become a Queen. And when she saw that Princess Velvet-Cheek was growing into a very beautiful young woman—more beautiful by far than her own daughter—she began to hate her, and to wish that in some way she would lose her good looks.

"For," thought she, "what suitor will heed my daughter as long as her step-sister is by her side?"

Now, among the servants and retainers at her husband's Castle there was an old Hen-wife, who, men said, was in league with the Evil Spirits of the air, and who was skilled in the knowledge of charms, and philtres, and love potions.

"Perhaps she could help me to do what I seek to do," said the wicked Queen; and one night, when it was growing dusk, she wrapped a cloak round her, and set out to this old Hen-wife's cottage.

"Send the lassie to me to-morrow morning ere she hath broken her fast," replied the old Dame when she heard what her visitor had to say. "I will find out a way to mar her beauty." And the wicked Queen went home content.

Next morning she went to the Princess's room while she was dressing, and told her to go out before breakfast and get the eggs that the Hen-wife had gathered. "And see," added she, "that thou dost not eat anything ere thou goest, for there is nothing that maketh the roses bloom on a young maiden's cheeks like going out fasting in the fresh morning air."

Princess Velvet-Cheek promised to do as she was bid, and go and fetch the eggs; but as she was not fond of going out of doors before she had had something to eat, and as, more-over, she suspected that her step-mother had some hidden reason for giving her such an unusual order, and she did not trust her step-mother's hidden reasons, she slipped into the pantry as she went downstairs and helped herself to a large slice of cake. Then, after she had eaten it, she went straight to the Hen-wife's cottage and asked for the eggs.

"Lift the lid of that pot there, your Highness, and you will see them," said the old woman, pointing to the big pot stand-ing in the corner in which she boiled her hens' meat.

The Princess did so, and found a heap of eggs lying in-side, which she lifted into her basket, while the old woman watched her with a curious smile.

"Go home to your Lady Mother, Hinny," she said at last, "and tell her from me to keep the press door better snibbit."

The Princess went home, and gave this extraordinary message to her step-mother, wondering to herself the while what it meant.

But if she did not understand the Hen-wife's words, the Queen understood them only too well. For from them she gathered that the Princess had in some way prevented the old Witch's spell doing what she intended it to do.

So next morning, when she sent her step-daughter once more on the same errand, she accompanied her to the door of the Castle herself, so that the poor girl had no chance of paying a visit to the pantry. But as she went along the road that led to the cottage, she felt so hungry that, when she passed a party of country-folk picking peas by the roadside, she asked them to give her a handful.

They did so, and she ate the peas; and so it came about that the same thing happened that had happened yesterday.

The Hen-wife sent her to look for the eggs; but she could work no spell upon her, because she had broken her fast. So the old woman bade her go home again and give the same message to the Queen.

The Queen was very angry when she heard it, for she felt that she was being outwitted by this slip of a girl, and she determined that, although she was not fond of getting up early, she would accompany her next day herself, and make sure that she had nothing to eat as she went.

So next morning she walked with the Princess to the Hen-wife's cottage, and, as had happened twice before, the old woman sent the Royal maiden to lift the lid off the pot in the corner in order to get the eggs.

And the moment that the Princess did so off jumped her own pretty head, and on jumped that of a sheep.

Then the wicked Queen thanked the cruel old Witch for the service that she had rendered to her, and went home quite delighted with the success of her scheme; while the poor Princess picked up her own head and put it into her basket along with the eggs, and went home crying, keeping behind the hedge all the way, for she felt so ashamed of her sheep's head that she was afraid that anyone saw her.

Now, as I told you, the Princess's step-sister Katherine loved her dearly, and when she saw what a cruel deed had been wrought on her she was so angry that she declared that she would not remain another hour in the Castle. "For," said she, "if my Lady Mother can order one such deed to be done, who can hinder her ordering another. So, methinks, 'twere better for us both to be where she cannot reach us."

So she wrapped a fine shawl round her poor step-sister's head, so that none could tell what it was like, and, putting the real head in the basket, she took her by the hand, and the two set out to seek their fortunes.

They walked and they walked, till they reached a splendid Palace, and when they came to it Katherine made as though she would go boldly up and knock at the door.

"I may perchance find work here," she explained, "and earn enough money to keep us both in comfort."

But the poor Princess would fain have pulled her back. "They will have nothing to do with thee," she whispered, "when they see that thou hast a sister with a sheep's head."

"And who is to know that thou hast a sheep's head?" asked Katherine. "If thou hold thy tongue, and keep the shawl well round thy face, and leave the rest to me."

So up she went and knocked at the kitchen door, and when the housekeeper came to answer it she asked her if there was any work that she could give her to do. "For," said she, "I have a sick sister, who is sore troubled with the migraine in her head, and I would fain find a quiet lodging for her where she could rest for the night."

"Dost thou know aught of sickness?" asked the housekeeper, who was greatly struck by Katherine's soft voice and gentle ways.

"Ay, do I," replied Katherine, "for when one's sister is troubled with the migraine, one has to learn to go about softly and not to make a noise."

Now it chanced that the King's eldest son, the Crown Prince, was lying ill in the Palace of a strange disease, which seemed to have touched his brain. For he was so restless, especially at nights, that someone had always to be with him to watch that he did himself no harm; and this state of things had gone on so long that everyone was quite worn out.

And the old housekeeper thought that it would be a good chance to get a quiet night's sleep if this capable-looking stranger could be trusted to sit up with the Prince.

So she left her at the door, and went and consulted the King; and the King came out and spoke to Katherine and he, too, was so pleased with her voice and her appearance that he gave orders that a room should be set apart in the Castle for her sick sister and herself, and he promised that, if she would sit up that night with the Prince, and see that no harm befell him, she would have, as her reward, a bag of silver Pennies in the morning.

Katherine agreed to the bargain readily, "for," thought she, "'twill always be a night's lodging for the Princess; and, forbye that, a bag of silver Pennies is not to be got every day."

So the Princess went to bed in the comfortable chamber that was set apart for her, and Katherine went to watch by the sick Prince.

He was a handsome, comely young man, who seemed to be in some sort of fever, for his brain was not quite clear, and he tossed and tumbled from side to side, gazing anxiously in front of him, and stretching out his hands as if he were in search of something.

And at twelve o'clock at night, just when Katherine thought that he was going to fall into a refreshing sleep, what was her horror to see him rise from his bed, dress himself hastily, open the door, and slip downstairs, as if he were going to look for somebody.

"There be something strange in this," said the girl to herself. "Methinks I had better follow him and see what happens."

So she stole out of the room after the Prince and followed him safely downstairs; and what was her astonishment to find that apparently he was going some distance, for he put on his hat and riding-coat, and, unlocking the door crossed the courtyard to the stable, and began to saddle his horse.

When he had done so, he led it out, and mounted, and, whistling softly to a hound which lay asleep in a corner, he prepared to ride away.

"I must go too, and see the end of this," said Katherine bravely; "for methinks he is bewitched. These be not the actions of a sick man."

So, just as the horse was about to start, she jumped lightly on its back, and settled herself comfortably behind its rider, all unnoticed by him.

Then this strange pair rode away through the woods, and, as they went, Katherine pulled the hazel-nuts that nodded in great clusters in her face. "For," said she to herself, "Dear only knows where next I may get anything to eat."

On and on they rode, till they left the greenwood far behind them and came out on an open moor. Soon they reached a hillock, and here the Prince drew rein, and, stooping down, cried in a strange, uncanny whisper, "Open, open, Green Hill, and let the Prince, and his horse, and his hound enter."

"And," whispered Katherine quickly, "let his lady enter behind him."

Instantly, to her great astonishment, the top of the knowe seemed to tip up, leaving an aperture large enough for the little company to enter; then it closed gently behind them again.

They found themselves in a magnificent hall, brilliantly lighted by hundreds of candles stuck in sconces round the walls. In the centre of this apartment was a group of the most beautiful maidens that Katherine had ever seen, all dressed in shimmering ball-gowns, with wreaths of roses and violets in their hair. And there were sprightly gallants also, who had been treading a measure with these beauteous damsels to the strains of fairy music.

When the maidens saw the Prince, they ran to him, and led him away to join their revels. And at the touch of their hands all his languor seemed to disappear, and he became the gayest of all the throng, and laughed, and danced, and sang as if he had never known what it was to be ill.

As no one took any notice of Katherine, she sat down quietly on a bit of rock to watch what would befall. And as she watched, she became aware of a wee, wee bairnie, playing with a tiny wand, quite close to her feet.

He was a bonnie bit bairn, and she was just thinking of trying to make friends with him when one of the beautiful maidens passed, and, looking at the wand, said to her partner, in a meaning tone, "Three strokes of that wand would give Katherine's sister back her pretty face."

Here was news indeed! Katherine's breath came thick and fast; and with trembling fingers she drew some of the nuts out of her pocket, and began rolling them carelessly towards the child. Apparently he did not get nuts very often, for he dropped his little wand at once, and stretched out his tiny hands to pick them up.

This was just what she wanted; and she slipped down from her seat to the ground, and drew a little nearer to him. Then she threw one or two more nuts in his way, and, when he was picking these up, she managed to lift the wand unobserved, and to hide it under her apron. After this, she crept cautiously back to her seat again; and not a moment too soon, for just then a cock crew, and at the sound the whole of the dancers vanished—all but the Prince, who ran to mount his horse, and was in such a hurry to be gone that Katherine had much ado to get up behind him before the hillock opened, and he rode swiftly into the outer world once more.

But she managed it, and, as they rode homewards in the grey morning light, she sat and cracked her nuts and ate them as fast as she could, for her adventures had made her marvellously hungry.

When she and her strange patient had once more reached the Castle, she just waited to see him go back to bed, and begin to toss and tumble as he had done before; then she ran to her step-sister's room, and, finding her asleep, with her poor misshapen head lying peacefully on the pillow, she gave it three sharp little strokes with the fairy wand and, lo and behold! the sheep's head vanished, and the Princess's own pretty one took its place.

In the morning the King and the old housekeeper came to inquire what kind of night the Prince had had. Katherine answered that he had had a very good night; for she was very anxious to stay with him longer, for now that she had found out that the Elfin Maidens who dwelt in the Green Knowe had thrown a spell over him, she was resolved to find out also how that spell could be loosed.

And Fortune favoured her; for the King was so pleased to think that such a suitable nurse had been found for the Prince, and he was also so charmed with the looks of her step-sister, who came out of her chamber as bright and bonnie as in the old days, declaring that her migraine was all gone, and that she was now able to do any work that the housekeeper might find for her, that he begged Katherine to stay with his son a little longer, adding that if she would do so, he would give her a bag of gold Bonnet Pieces.

So Katherine agreed readily; and that night she watched by the Prince as she had done the night before. And at twelve o'clock he rose and dressed himself, and rode to the Fairy Knowe, just as she had expected him to do, for she was quite certain that the poor young man was bewitched, and not suffering from a fever, as everyone thought he was.

And you may be sure that she accompanied him, riding behind him all unnoticed, and filling her pockets with nuts as she rode.

When they reached the Fairy Knowe, he spoke the same words that he had spoken the night before. "Open, open, Green Hill, and let the young Prince in with his horse and his hound." And when the Green Hill opened, Katherine added softly, "And his lady behind him." So they all passed in together.

Katherine seated herself on a stone, and looked around her. The same revels were going on as yesternight, and the Prince was soon in the thick of them, dancing and laughing madly. The girl watched him narrowly, wondering if she would ever be able to find out what would restore him to his right mind; and, as she was watching him, the same little bairn who had played with the magic wand came up to her again. Only this time he was playing with a little bird.

And as he played, one of the dancers passed by, and, turning to her partner, said lightly, "Three bites of that birdie would lift the Prince's sickness, and make him as well as he ever was." Then she joined in the dance again, leaving Katherine sitting upright on her stone quivering with excitement.

If only she could get that bird the Prince might be cured! Very carefully she began to shake some nuts out of her pocket, and roll them across the floor towards the child.

He picked them up eagerly, letting go the bird as he did so; and, in an instant, Katherine caught it, and hid it under her apron.

In no long time after that the cock crew, and the Prince

and she set out on their homeward ride. But this morning, instead of cracking nuts, she killed and plucked the bird, scattering its feathers all along the road; and the instant she gained the Prince's room, and had seen him safely into bed, she put it on a spit in front of the fire and began to roast it.

And soon it began to frizzle, and get brown, and smell deliciously, and the Prince, in his bed in the corner, opened his eyes and murmured faintly, "How I wish I had a bite of that birdie."

When she heard the words Katherine's heart jumped for joy, and as soon as the bird was roasted she cut a little piece from its breast and popped it into the Prince's mouth.

When he had eaten it his strength seemed to come back somewhat, for he rose on his elbow and looked at his nurse. "Oh! if I had but another bite of that birdie!" he said. And his voice was certainly stronger.

So Katherine gave him another piece, and when he had eaten that he sat right up in bed.

"Oh! if I had but a third bite o' that birdie!" he cried. And now the colour was coming back into his face, and his eyes were shining.

This time Katherine brought him the whole of the rest of the bird; and he ate it up greedily, picking the bones quite clean with his fingers; and when it was finished, he sprang out of bed and dressed himself, and sat down by the fire.

And when the King came in the morning, with his old housekeeper at his back, to see how the Prince was, he found him sitting cracking nuts with his nurse, for Katherine had brought home quite a lot in her apron pocket.

The King was so delighted to find his son cured that he

gave all the credit to Katherine Crackernuts, as he called her, and he gave orders at once that the Prince should marry her. "For," said he, "a maiden who is such a good nurse is sure to make a good Queen."

The Prince was quite willing to do as his father bade him; and, while they were talking together, his younger brother came in, leading Princess Velvet-Cheek by the hand, whose acquaintance he had made but yesterday, declaring that he had fallen in love with her, and that he wanted to marry her immediately.

So it all fell out very well, and everybody was quite pleased; and the two weddings took place at once, and, unless they be dead sinsyne, the young couples are living yet.

THE WELL O' THE
WORLD'S END

There was once an old widow woman, who lived in a little cottage with her only daughter, who was such a bonnie lassie that everyone liked to look at her.

One day the old woman took a notion into her head to bake a girdleful of cakes. So she took down her bakeboard, and went to the girnel and fetched a basinful of meal; but when she went to seek a jug of water to mix the meal with, she found that there was none in the house.

So she called to her daughter, who was in the garden; and when the girl came she held out the empty jug to her, saying, "Run, like a good lassie, to the Well o' the World's End and bring me a jug of water, for I have long found that water from the Well o' the World's End makes the best cakes."

So the lassie took the jug and set out on her errand.

Now, as its name shows, it is a long road to that well, and many a weary mile had the poor maid to go ere she reached it.

But she arrived there at last; and what was her disappointment to find it dry.

She was so tired and so vexed that she sat down beside it and began to cry; for she did not know where to get any more water, and she felt that she could not go back to her mother with an empty jug.

While she was crying, a nice yellow Paddock, with very bright eyes, came jump-jump-jumping over the stones of the well, and squatted down at her feet, looking up into her face.

"And why are ye greeting, my bonnie maid?" he asked. "Is there aught that I can do to help thee?"

"I am greeting because the well is empty," she answered,

"and I cannot get any water to carry home to my mother."

"Listen," said the Paddock softly. "I can get thee water in plenty, if so be thou wilt promise to be my wife."

Now the lassie had but one thought in her head, and that was to get the water for her mother's oat-cakes, and she never for a moment thought that the Paddock was in earnest, so she promised gladly enough to be his wife, if he would get her a jug of water.

No sooner had the words passed her lips than the beastie jumped down the mouth of the well, and in another moment it was full to the brim with water.

The lassie filled her jug and carried it home, without troubling any more about the matter. But late that night, just as her mother and she were going to bed, something came with a faint "thud, thud," against the cottage door, and then they heard a tiny little wee voice singing:

> *"Oh, open the door, my hinnie, my heart,*
> *Oh, open the door, my ain true love;*
> *Remember the promise that you and I made*
> *Down i' the meadow, where we two met."*

"Wheesht," said the old woman, raising her head. "What noise is that at the door?"

"Oh," said her daughter, who was feeling rather frightened, "it's only a yellow Paddock."

"Poor bit beastie," said the kind-hearted old mother. "Open the door and let him in. It's cold work sitting on the doorstep."

So the lassie, very unwillingly opened the door, and the Paddock came jump-jump-jumping across the kitchen, and sat down at the fireside.

And while he sat there he began to sing this song:

> *"Oh, gie me my supper, my hinnie, my heart,*
> *Oh, gie me my supper, my ain true love;*
> *Remember the promise that you and I made*
> *Down i' the meadow, where we two met."*

"Gie the poor beast his supper," said the old woman. "He's an uncommon Paddock that can sing like that."

"Tut," replied her daughter crossly, for she was growing more and more frightened as she saw the creature's bright black eyes fixed on her face. "I'm not going to be so silly as to feed a wet, sticky Paddock."

"Don't be ill-natured and cruel," said her mother. "Who knows how far the little beastie has travelled? And I warrant that it would like a saucerful of milk."

Now, the lassie could have told her that the Paddock had travelled from the Well o' the World's End; but she held her tongue, and went ben to the milk-house, and brought back a saucerful of milk, which she set down before the strange little visitor.

> *"Now chap off my head, my hinnie, my heart,*
> *Now chap off my head, my ain true love,*
> *Remember the promise that you and I made*
> *Down i' the meadow, where we two met."*

"Hout, havers, pay no heed, the creature's daft," exclaimed the old woman, running forward to stop her daughter, who was raising the axe to chop off the Paddock's head.

But she was too late; down came the axe, off went the head; and lo, and behold! on the spot where the little creature had sat, stood the handsomest young Prince that had ever been seen.

He wore such a noble air, and was so richly dressed, that the astonished girl and her mother would have fallen on their knees before him had he not prevented them by a movement of his hand.

"'Tis I that should kneel to thee, Sweetheart," he said, turning to the blushing girl, "for thou hast delivered me from a fearful spell, which was cast over me in my infancy by a wicked Fairy, who at the same time slew my father. For long years I have lived in that well, the Well o' the World's End, waiting for a maiden to appear, who should take pity on me, even in my loathsome disguise, and promise to be my wife, and who would also have the kindness to let me into her house, and the courage, at my bidding, to cut off my head.

"Now I can return and claim my father's Kingdom, and thou, most gracious maiden, will go with me, and be my bride, for thou well deserv'st the honour."

And this was how the lassie who went to fetch water from the Well o' the World's End became a Princess.

FARQUHAR MACNEILL

Once upon a time there was a young man named Farquhar MacNeill. He had just gone to a new situation, and the very first night after he went to it his mistress asked him if he would go over the hill to the house of a neighbour and borrow a sieve, for her own was all in holes, and she wanted to sift some meal.

Farquhar agreed to do so, for he was a willing lad, and he set out at once upon his errand, after the farmer's wife had pointed out to him the path that he was to follow, and told him that he would have no difficulty in finding the house, even though it was strange to him, for he would be sure to see the light in the window.

He had not gone very far, however, before he saw what he took to be the light from a cottage window on his left hand, some distance from the path, and, forgetting his Mistress's instructions that he was to follow the path right over the hill, he left it, and walked towards the light.

It seemed to him that he had almost reached it when his foot tripped, and he fell down, down, down, into a Fairy Parlour, far under the ground.

It was full of Fairies, who were engaged in different occupations.

Close by the door, or rather the hole down which he had so unceremoniously tumbled, two little elderly women, in black aprons and white mutches, were busily engaged in grinding corn between two flat millstones. Other two Fairies, younger women, in blue print gowns and white kerchiefs, were gathering up the freshly ground meal, and baking it into bannocks, which they were toasting on a girdle over a peat fire, which was burning slowly in a corner.

In the centre of the large apartment a great troop of Fairies, Elves, and Sprites were dancing reels as hard as they could to the music of a tiny set of bagpipes which were being played by a brown-faced Gnome, who sat on a ledge of rock far above their heads.

They all stopped their various employments when Farquhar came suddenly down in their midst, and looked at him in alarm; but when they saw that he was not hurt, they bowed gravely and bade him be seated. Then they went on with their work and with their play as if nothing had happened.

But Farquhar, being very fond of dancing, and being in no wise anxious to be seated, thought that he would like to have a reel first, so he asked the Fairies if he might join them. And they, although they looked surprised at his request, allowed him to do so, and in a few minutes the young man was dancing away as gaily as any of them.

And as he danced a strange change came over him. He forgot his errand, he forgot his home, he forgot everything that had ever happened to him, he only knew that he wanted to remain with the Fairies all the rest of his life.

And he did remain with them—for a magic spell had been cast over him, and he became like one of themselves, and could come and go at nights without being seen, and could sip the dew from the grass and honey from the flowers as daintily and noiselessly as if he had been a Fairy born.

Time passed by, and one night he and a band of merry companions set out for a long journey through the air. They started early, for they intended to pay a visit to the Man in the Moon and be back again before cock-crow.

All would have gone well if Farquhar had only looked where he was going, but he did not, being deeply engaged in making love to a young Fairy Maiden by his side, so he never saw a cottage that was standing right in his way, till he struck against the chimney and stuck fast in the thatch.

His companions sped merrily on, not noticing what had befallen him, and he was left to disentangle himself as best he could.

As he was doing so he chanced to glance down the wide chimney, and in the cottage kitchen he saw a comely young woman dandling a rosy-cheeked baby.

Now, when Farquhar had been in his mortal state, he had been very fond of children, and a word of blessing rose to his lips.

"God shield thee," he said, as he looked at the mother and child, little guessing what the result of his words would be.

For scarce had the Holy Name crossed his lips than the spell which had held him so long was broken, and he became as he had been before.

Instantly his thoughts flew to his friends at home, and to the new Mistress whom he had left waiting for her sieve; for he felt sure that some weeks must have elapsed since he set out to fetch it. So he made haste to go to the farm.

When he arrived in the neighbourhood everything seemed strange. There were woods where no woods used to be, and walls where no walls used to be. To his amazement, he could not find his way to the farm, and, worst of all, in the place where he expected to find his father's house he found nothing but a crop of rank green nettles.

In great distress he looked about for someone to tell him what it all meant, and at last he found an old man thatching the roof of a cottage.

This old man was so thin and grey that at first Farquhar took him for a patch of mist, but as he went nearer he saw that he was a human being, and, going close up to the wall and shouting with all his might, for he felt sure that such an ancient man would be deaf, he asked him if he could tell him where his friends had gone to, and what had happened to his father's dwelling.

The old man listened, then he shook his head. "I never heard of him," he answered slowly; "but perhaps my father might be able to tell you."

"Your father!" said Farquhar, in great surprise. "Is it possible that your father is alive?"

"Aye he is," answered the old man, with a little laugh. "If you go into the house you'll find him sitting in the arm-chair by the fire."

Farquhar did as he was bid, and on entering the cottage found another old man, who was so thin and withered and bent that he looked as if he must at least be a hundred years old. He was feebly twisting ropes to bind the thatch on the roof.

"Can ye tell me aught of my friends, or where my father's cottage is?" asked Farquhar again, hardly expecting that this second old man would be able to answer him.

"I cannot," mumbled this ancient person; "but perhaps my father can tell you."

"Your father!" exclaimed Farquhar, more astonished than ever. "But surely he must be dead long ago."

The old man shook his head with a weird grimace.

"Look there," he said, and pointed with a twisted finger, to a leathern purse, or sporran, which was hanging to one of the posts of a wooden bedstead in the corner.

Farquhar approached it, and was almost frightened out of his wits by seeing a tiny shrivelled face crowned by a red pirnie, looking over the edge of the sporran.

"Tak' him out; he'll no touch ye," chuckled the old man by the fire.

So Farquhar took the little creature out carefully between his finger and thumb, and set him on the palm of his left hand. He was so shrivelled with age that he looked just like a mummy.

"Dost know anything of my friends, or where my father's cottage is gone to?" asked Farquhar for the third time, hardly expecting to get an answer.

"They were all dead long before I was born," piped out the tiny figure. "I never saw any of them, but I have heard my father speak of them."

"Then I must be older than you!" cried Farquhar, in great dismay. And he got such a shock at the thought that his bones suddenly dissolved into dust, and he fell, a heap of grey ashes, on the floor.

PEERIFOOL

There was once a King and a Queen in Rousay who had three daughters. When the young Princesses were just grown up, the King died, and the Crown passed to a distant cousin, who had always hated him, and who paid no heed to the widowed Queen and her daughters.

So they were left very badly off, and they went to live in a tiny cottage, and did all the housework themselves. They had a kailyard in front of the cottage, and a little field behind it, and they had a cow that grazed in the field, and which they fed with the cabbages that grew in the kailyard. For everyone knows that to feed cows with cabbages makes them give a larger quantity of milk.

But they soon discovered that some one was coming at night and stealing the cabbages, and, of course, this annoyed them very much. For they knew that if they had not cabbages to give to the cow, they would not have enough milk to sell.

So the eldest Princess said she would take out a three-legged stool, and wrap herself in a blanket, and sit in the kailyard all night to see if she could catch the thief. And, although it was very cold and very dark, she did so.

At first it seemed as if all her trouble would be in vain, for hour after hour passed and nothing happened. But in the small hours of the morning, just as the clock was striking two, she heard a stealthy trampling in the field behind, as if some very heavy person were trying to tread very softly, and presently a mighty Giant stepped right over the wall into the kailyard.

He carried an enormous creel on his arm, and a large, sharp knife in his hand; and he began to cut the cabbages, and to throw them into the creel as fast as he could.

Now the Princess was no coward, so, although she had not expected to face a Giant, she gathered up her courage, and cried out sharply, "Who gave thee liberty to cut our cabbages? Leave off this minute, and go away."

The Giant paid no heed, but went on steadily with what he was doing.

"Dost thou not hear me?" cried the girl indignantly; for she was the Princess Royal, and had always been accustomed to be obeyed.

"If thou be not quiet I will take thee too," said the Giant grimly, pressing the cabbages down into the creel.

"I should like to see thee try," retorted the Princess, rising from her stool and stamping her foot; for she felt so angry that she forgot for a moment that she was only a weak maiden and he was a great and powerful Giant.

And, as if to show her how strong he was, he seized her by her arm and her leg, and put her in his creel on the top of the cabbages, and carried her away bodily.

When he reached his home, which was in a great square house on a lonely moor, he took her out, and set her down roughly on the floor.

"Thou wilt be my servant now," he said, "and keep my house, and do my errands for me. I have a cow, which thou must drive out every day to the hillside; and see, here is a bag of wool, when thou hast taken out the cow, thou must come back and settle thyself at home, as a good housewife should, and comb, and card it, and spin it into yarn, with which to weave a good thick cloth for my raiment. I am out most of the day, but when I come home I shall expect to find all this done, and a great bicker of porridge boiled besides for my supper."

The poor Princess was very dismayed when she heard these words, for she had never been accustomed to work hard, and she had always had her sisters to help her; but the Giant took no notice of her distress, but went out as soon as it was daylight, leaving her alone in the house to begin her work.

As soon as he had gone she drove the cow to the pasture, as he had told her to do; but she had a good long walk over the moor before she reached the hill, and by the time that she got back to the house she felt very tired.

So she thought that she would put on the porridge pot, and make herself some porridge before she began to card and comb the wool. She did so, and just as she was sitting down to sup them the door opened, and a crowd of wee, wee Peerie Folk came in.

They were the tiniest men and women that the Princess had ever seen; not one of them would have reached half-way to her knee; and they were dressed in dresses fashioned out of all the colours of the rainbow—scarlet and blue, green and yellow, orange and violet; and the funny thing was, that every one of them had a shock of straw-coloured yellow hair.

They were all talking and laughing with one another; and they hopped up, first on stools, then on chairs, till at last they reached the top of the table, where they clustered round the bowl, out of which the Princess was eating her porridge.

"We be hungry, we be hungry," they cried, in their tiny shrill voices. "Spare a little porridge for the Peerie Folk."

But the Princess was hungry also; and, besides being hungry, she was both tired and cross; so she shook her head and waved them impatiently away with her spoon,

"Little for one, and less for two,
And never a grain have I for you."

she said sharply, and, to her great delight, for she did not feel quite comfortable with all the Peerie Folk standing on the table looking at her, they vanished in a moment.

After this she finished her porridge in peace; then she took the wool out of the bag, and she set to work to comb and card it. But it seemed as if it were bewitched; it curled and twisted and coiled itself round her fingers so that, try as she would, she could not do anything with it. And when the Giant came home he found her sitting in despair with it all in confusion round her, and the porridge, which she had left for him in the pot, burned to a cinder.

As you may imagine, he was very angry, and raged, and stamped, and used the most dreadful words; and at last he took her by the heels, and beat her until all her back was skinned and bleeding; then he carried her out to the byre, and threw her up on the joists among the hens. And, although she was not dead, she was so stunned and bruised that she could only lie there motionless, looking down on the backs of the cows.

Time went on, and in the kailyard at home the cabbages were disappearing as fast as ever. So the second Princess said that she would do as her sister had done, and wrap herself in a blanket, and go and sit on a three-legged stool all night, to see what was becoming of them.

She did so, and exactly the same fate befell her that had befallen her elder sister. The Giant appeared with his creel, and he carried her off, and set her to mind the cow and the house, and to make his porridge and to spin; and the little yellow-headed Peerie Folk appeared and asked her for some supper, and she refused to give it to them; and after that, she could not comb or card her wool, and the Giant was angry, and he scolded her, and beat her, and threw her up, half dead, on the joists beside her sister and the hens.

Then the youngest Princess determined to sit out in the kailyard all night, not so much to see what was becoming of the cabbages, as to discover what had happened to her sisters.

And when the Giant came and carried her off, she was not at all sorry, but very glad, for she was a brave and loving little maiden; and now she felt that she had a chance of finding out where they were, and whether they were dead or alive.

So she was quite cheerful and happy, for she felt certain that she was clever enough to outwit the Giant, if only she were watchful and patient; so she lay quite quietly in her creel above the cabbages, but she kept her eyes very wide open to see by which road he was carrying her off.

And when he set her down in his kitchen, and told her all that he expected her to do, she did not look downcast like her sisters, but nodded her head brightly, and said that she felt sure that she could do it.

And she sang to herself as she drove the cow over the moor to pasture, and she ran the whole way back, so that she should have a good long afternoon to work at the wool, and, although she would not have told the Giant this, to search the house.

Before she set to work, however, she made herself some porridge, just as her sisters had done; and, just as she was going to sup them, all the little yellow-haired Peerie Folk trooped in, and climbed up on the table, and stood and stared at her.

"We be hungry, we be hungry," they cried. "Spare a little

porridge for the Peerie Folk."

"With all my heart," replied the good-natured Princess. "If you can find dishes little enough for you to sup out of, I will fill them for you. But, methinks, if I were to give you all porringers, you would smother yourselves among the porridge."

At her words the Peerie Folk shouted with laughter, till their straw-coloured hair tumbled right over their faces; then they hopped on to the floor and ran out of the house, and presently they came trooping back holding cups of blue-bells, and foxgloves, and saucers of primroses and anemones in their hands; and the Princess put a tiny spoonful of porridge into each saucer, and a tiny drop of milk into each cup, and they ate it all up as daintily as possible with neat little grass spoons, which they had brought with them in their pockets.

When they had finished they all cried out, "Thank you! Thank you!" and ran out of the kitchen again, leaving the Princess alone. And, being alone, she went all over the house to look for her sisters, but, of course, she could not find them.

"Never mind, I will find them soon," she said to herself. "To-morrow I will search the byre and the outhouses; in the meantime, I had better get on with my work." So she went back to the kitchen, and took out the bag of wool, which the Giant had told her to make into cloth.

But just as she was doing so the door opened once more, and a Yellow-Haired Peerie Boy entered. He was exactly like the other Peerie Folk who had eaten the Princess's porridge, only he was bigger, and he wore a very rich dress of grass-green velvet. He walked boldly into the middle of the kitchen and looked round him.

"Hast thou any work for me to do?" he asked. "I ken grand how to handle wool and turn it into fine thick cloth."

"I have plenty of work for anybody who asks it," replied the Princess; "but I have no money to pay for it, and there are but few folk in this world who will work without wages."

"All the wages that I ask is that thou wilt take the trouble to find out my name, for few folk ken it, and few folk care to ken. But if by any chance thou canst not find it out, then must thou pay toll of half of thy cloth."

The Princess thought that it would be quite an easy thing to find out the Boy's name, so she agreed to the bargain, and, putting all the wool back into the bag, she gave it to him, and he swung it over his shoulder and departed.

She ran to the door to see where he went, for she had made up her mind that she would follow him secretly to his home, and find out from the neighbours what his name was.

But, to her great dismay, though she looked this way and that, he had vanished completely, and she began to wonder what she should do if the Giant came back and found that she had allowed someone, whose name she did not even know, to carry off all the wool.

And, as the afternoon wore on, and she could think of no way of finding out who the boy was, or where he came from, she felt that she had made a great mistake, and she began to grow very frightened.

Just as the gloaming was beginning to fall a knock came at the door, and, when she opened it, she found an old woman standing outside, who begged for a night's lodging.

Now, as I have told you, the Princess was very kind-hearted, and she would fain have granted the poor old Dame's request, but she dared not, for she did not know what the Giant would say. So she told the old woman that she could not take her in for the night, as she was only a servant, and not the mistress of the house; but she made her sit down on a bench beside the door, and brought her out some bread and milk, and gave her some water to bathe her poor, tired feet.

She was so bonnie, and gentle, and kind, and she looked so sorry when she told her that she would need to turn her away, that the old woman gave her her blessing, and told her not to vex herself, as it was a fine, dry night, and now that she had had a meal she could easily sit down somewhere and sleep in the shelter of the outhouses.

And, when she had finished her bread and milk, she went and laid down by the side of a green knowe, which rose out of the moor not very far from the byre door.

And, strange to say, as she lay there she felt the earth beneath her getting warmer and warmer, until she was so hot that she was fain to crawl up the side of the hillock, in the hope of getting a mouthful of fresh air.

And as she got near the top she heard a voice, which seemed to come from somewhere beneath her, saying, "TEASE, TEASENS, TEASE; CARD, CARDENS, CARD; SPIN, SPINNENS, SPIN; for PEERIFOOL PEERIFOOL, PEERI-FOOL is what men call me." And when she got to the very top, she found that there was a crack in the earth, through which rays of light were coming; and when she put her eye to the crack, what should she see down below her but a brilliantly lighted chamber, in which all the Peerie Folk were sitting in a circle, working away as hard as they could.

Some of them were carding wool, some of them were combing it, some of them were spinning it, constantly wetting their fingers with their lips, in order to twist the yarn fine as they drew it from the distaff, and some of them were spinning the yarn into cloth.

While round and round the circle, cracking a little whip, and urging them to work faster, was a Yellow-Haired Peerie Boy.

"This is a strange thing, and these be queer on-goings," said the old woman to herself, creeping hastily down to the bottom of the hillock again. "I must e'en go and tell the bonnie lassie in the house yonder. Maybe the knowledge of what I have seen will stand her in good stead some day. When there be Peerie Folk about, it is well to be on one's guard."

So she went back to the house and told the Princess all that she had seen and heard, and the Princess was so delighted with what she had told her that she risked the Giant's wrath and allowed her to go and sleep in the hayloft.

It was not very long after the old woman had gone to rest before the door opened, and the Peerie Boy appeared once more with a number of webs of cloth upon his shoulder. "Here is thy cloth," he said, with a sly smile, "and I will put it on the shelf for thee the moment that thou tellest me what my name is."

Then the Princess, who was a merry maiden, thought that she would tease the little follow for a time ere she let him know that she had found out his secret.

So she mentioned first one name and then another, always pretending to think that she had hit upon the right one; and all the time the Peerie Boy jumped from side to side with delight, for he thought that she would never find out the right name, and that half of the cloth would be his.

But at last the Princess grew tired of joking, and she cried out, with a little laugh of triumph, "Dost thou by any chance ken anyone called PEERIFOOL, little Mannikin?"

Then he knew that in some way she had found out what

men called him, and he was so angry and disappointed that he flung the webs of cloth down in a heap on the floor, and ran out at the door, slamming it behind him.

Meanwhile the Giant was coming down the hill in the darkening, and, to his astonishment, he met a troop of little Peerie Folk toiling up it, looking as if they were so tired that they could hardly get along. Their eyes were dim and listless, their heads were hanging on their breasts, and their lips were so long and twisted that the poor little people looked quite hideous.

The Giant asked how this was, and they told him that they had to work so hard all day, spinning for their Master that they were quite exhausted; and that the reason why their lips were so distorted was that they used them constantly to wet their fingers, so that they might pull the wool in very fine strands from the distaff.

"I always thought a great deal of women who could spin," said the Giant, "and I looked out for a housewife that could do so. But after this I will be more careful, for the housewife that I have now is a bonnie little woman, and I would be loth to have her spoil her face in that manner."

And he hurried home in a great state of mind in case he should find that his new servant's pretty red lips had grown long and ugly in his absence.

Great was his relief to see her standing by the table, bonnie and winsome as ever, with all the webs of cloth in a pile in front of her.

"By my troth, thou art an industrious maiden," he said, in high good humour, "and, as a reward for working so diligently, I will restore thy sisters to thee." And he went out to the byre, and lifted the two other Princesses down from the rafters, and brought them in and laid them on the settle.

Their little sister nearly screamed aloud when she saw how ill they looked and how bruised their backs were, but, like a prudent maiden, she held her tongue, and busied herself with applying a cooling ointment to their wounds, and binding them up, and by and by her sisters revived, and, after the Giant had gone to bed, they told her all that had befallen them.

"I will be avenged on him for his cruelty," said the little Princess firmly; and when she spoke like that her sisters knew that she meant what she said.

So next morning, before the Giant was up, she fetched his creel, and put her eldest sister into it, and covered her with all the fine silken hangings and tapestry that she could find, and on the top of all she put a handful of grass, and when the Giant came downstairs she asked him, in her sweetest tone, if he would do her a favour.

And the Giant, who was very pleased with her because of the quantity of cloth which he thought she had spun, said that he would.

"Then carry that creelful of grass home to my mother's cottage for her cow to eat," said the Princess. "'Twill help to make up for all the cabbages which thou hast stolen from her kailyard."

And, wonderful to relate, the Giant did as he was bid, and carried the creel to the cottage.

Next morning she put her second sister into another creel, and covered her with all the fine napery she could find in the house, and put an armful of grass on the top of it, and at her bidding the Giant, who was really getting very fond of her, carried it also home to her mother.

The next morning the little Princess told him that she

thought that she would go for a long walk after she had done her housework, and that she might not be in when he came home at night, but that she would have another creel of grass ready for him, if he would carry it to the cottage as he had done on the two previous evenings. He promised to do so; then, as usual, he went out for the day.

In the afternoon the clever little maiden went through the house, gathering together all the lace, and silver, and jewellery that she could find, and brought them and placed them beside the creel. Then she went out and cut an armful of grass, and brought it in and laid it beside them.

Then she crept into the creel herself, and pulled all the fine things in above her, and then she covered everything up with the grass, which was a very difficult thing to do, seeing she herself was at the bottom of the basket. Then she lay quite still and waited.

Presently the Giant came in, and, obedient to his promise, he lifted the creel and carried it off to the old Queen's cottage.

No one seemed to be at home, so he set it down in the entry, and turned to go away. But the little Princess had told her sisters what to do, and they had a great can of boiling water ready in one of the rooms upstairs, and when they heard his steps coming round that side of the house, they threw open the window and emptied it all over his head; and that was the end of him.

THE MERMAID WIFE

A story is told of an inhabitant of Unst, who, in walking on the sandy margin of a voe, saw a number of mermen and mermaids dancing by moonlight, and several seal-skins strewed beside them on the ground. At his approach they immediately fled to secure their garbs, and, taking upon themselves the form of seals, plunged immediately into the sea. But as the Shetlander perceived that one skin lay close to his feet, he snatched it up, bore it swiftly away, and placed it in concealment. On returning to the shore he met the fairest damsel that was ever gazed upon by mortal eyes, lamenting the robbery, by which she had become an exile from her submarine friends, and a tenant of the upper world. Vainly she implored the restitution of her property; the man had drunk deeply of love, and was inexorable; but he offered her protection beneath his roof as his betrothed spouse. The merlady, perceiving that she must become an inhabitant of the earth, found that she could not do better than accept of the offer. This strange attachment subsisted for many years, and the couple had several children. The Shetlander's love for his merwife was unbounded, but his affection was coldly returned. The lady would often steal alone to the desert strand, and, on a signal being given, a large seal would make his appearance, with whom she would hold, in an unknown tongue, an anxious conference. Years had thus glided away, when it happened that one of the children, in the course of his play, found concealed beneath a stack of corn a seal's skin; and, delighted with the prize, he ran with it to his mother. Her eyes glistened with rapture--she gazed upon it as her own--as the means by which she could pass through the ocean that led to her native home. She burst forth into an ecstasy of joy, which was only moderated when she beheld her children, whom she was now about to leave; and, after hastily embracing them, she fled with all speed towards the sea-side. The husband immediately returned, learned the discovery that had taken place, ran to overtake his wife, but only arrived in time to see her transformation of shape completed--to see her, in the form of a seal, bound from the ledge of a rock into the sea. The large animal of the same kind with whom she had held a secret converse soon appeared, and evidently congratulated her, in the most tender manner, on her escape. But before she dived to unknown depths, she cast a parting glance at the wretched Shetlander, whose despairing looks excited in her breast a few transient feelings of commiseration.

"Farewell!" said she to him, "and may all good attend you. I loved you very well when I resided upon earth, but I always loved my first husband much better."

www.sophenebooks.com

SOPHENE